"You

Susan said—and it was the hardest thing she'd ever had to say.

"I'm not going to forget you, and you're not going to forget me, either," Haggerty answered heatedly.

Susan tried to imagine what Steffie, the woman she was pretending to be, would say in this situation. She forced a note of sarcasm into her voice. "The trouble with big strong men is the big strong egos that go along with them. What's wrong, Haggerty? Have a problem with the idea that kissing you wasn't a milestone in my life?"

"You're good, lady, really good. You're going to pretend that this...whatever it is...between us doesn't exist."

"We'll just have to ignore it," Susan said, the words catching in her throat.

"We've tried that, Steffie. It didn't work!"

Dear Reader,

Welcome to Silhouette. Experience the magic of the wonderful world where two people fall in love. Meet heroines who will make you cheer for their happiness, and heroes (be they the boy next door or a handsome, mysterious stranger) who will win your heart. Silhouette Romances reflect the magic of love—sweeping you away with books that will make you laugh and cry, heartwarming, poignant stories that will move you time and time again.

In the next few months, we're publishing romances by many of your all-time favorites, such as Diana Palmer, Brittany Young, Emilie Richards and Arlene James. Your response to these authors and other authors of Silhouette Romances has served as a touchstone for us, and we're pleased to bring you more books with Silhouette's distinctive medley of charm, wit and—above all—*romance*.

I hope you enjoy this book and the many stories to come. Experience the magic!

Sincerely,

Tara Hughes
Senior Editor
Silhouette Books

GLENDA SANDS
Logan's Woman

Silhouette Romance

Published by Silhouette Books New York

America's Publisher of Contemporary Romance

SILHOUETTE BOOKS
300 E. 42nd St., New York, N.Y. 10017

Copyright © 1987 by Glenda Sands

All rights reserved, including the right to reproduce
this book or portions thereof in any form whatsoever.
For information address Silhouette Books,
300 E. 42nd St., New York, N.Y. 10017

ISBN: 0-373-08496-X

First Silhouette Books printing April 1987

All the characters in this book are fictitious. Any
resemblance to actual persons, living or dead, is
purely coincidental.

SILHOUETTE, SILHOUETTE ROMANCE and colophon
are registered trademarks of the publisher.

America's Publisher of Contemporary Romance

Printed in the U.S.A.

GLENDA SANDS's

feature writing career led her to cow lots and campaign trails, chimney sweeps and cookie entrepreneurs before she, as she puts it, "stumbled onto the primrose path of fiction." A native Texan, Ms. Sands lives in Houston with her husband and two children.

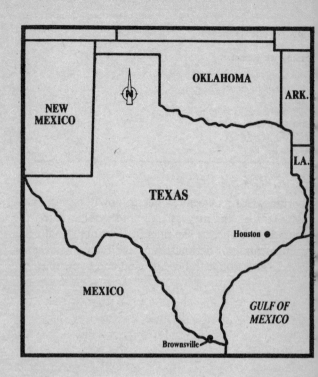

Chapter One

Curtain time in ten minutes, Susan Carlson thought. Thanks to the hours she'd spent behind the wheel practicing, she managed to downshift the Corvette and steer it onto the freeway exit ramp without a single lurch. If only the rest of the day could progress as smoothly....

Under the hood, the Corvette's powerful engine whined in protest at being slowed down, as if it, too, were in a hurry to reach the Logan International Freight Transport warehouse. High-octane gasoline was making the car's engine purr; Susan was running on the adrenaline of anticipation. She, Susan Patricia Owens Carlson—widow of Greg Carlson, mother of Kara and Greg Junior, drudge to a forty-hour-per-week government job monitoring tourists crossing the border from Mexico to the United States—was on the verge of entering into international intrigue.

A mile or so up the asphalt road the company's initials, LIFT, in red letters on a black rectangle fifteen feet high and thirty feet wide identified the entrance to the Logan International warehouse complex. As Susan steered the Corvette into the lot, a wave of panic seized her. What was she doing in Houston in a sports car pretending to be someone else? Jumping frijoles, what had she gotten herself into?

Peter Warshauer, the U.S. Drug Task Force agent who had recruited her, had made it sound simple when he'd approached her about the assignment. "The resemblance between you and this Steffie Meeks is uncanny. A few cosmetic changes and you'll be a dead ringer. Logan himself wouldn't be able to tell you apart."

"A few cosmetic changes?" she'd protested, too late. A trip to an expensive styling salon had been part of the carrot Peter had dangled in front of her. He'd mentioned the expensive kit of designer cosmetics she would be trained to use. He hadn't mentioned that her ash-blond shoulder-length hair would be bobbed to chin length, layered on top and dyed an exotic color called apricot fizz. Nor had he mentioned the green contact lenses that would disguise the blue of her eyes. Now when she peered in a mirror, a glamorous, exotic stranger peered back.

Victor Logan's reserved parking space, the closest to the employee entrance of the warehouse, was marked with a bright white sign with glossy black block lettering. Susan pulled the Corvette into the space and cut off the engine. For almost a minute she made no move to leave the car as she battled the stage fright that made her want to recrank the engine and drive as far away from the warehouse as possible. Then, after fortifying herself with a sharp intake of breath, she slipped the strap of Steffie Meeks's snakeskin portfolio over her shoulders, squared them and walked toward the warehouse with a determined stride.

The heavy steel door opened more easily than she expected. She stepped onto the concrete floor of the warehouse, letting the door whoosh closed behind her, and scanned the cavernous room to get her bearings. Crates of wood or metal and corrugated cardboard boxes of varying size dotted the storage area, seemingly without logical order. At the far side of the building, visible only through the angular skyline of crate tops, a bright rectangle of light proved the loading dock was where the sketches had indicated it would be. Profiled by the light, an unattended forklift looked like some bizarre demon from a B-grade horror movie.

Directly across the room from where Susan was standing, strips of fluorescent lighting shone brightly through the large windows of two offices perched on a loft that overlooked the storage area. Victor Logan's office, where she would be working, was the one on the left. She studied the position of the door in relation to the top of the stairs. A mistake as stupid as walking to the wrong office would be disastrous.

Movement in the office adjacent to Logan's attracted her attention, and she looked over to discover a man passing through the doorway of that office and onto the loft landing. A large man with dark hair—that would be Clark Haggerty, the warehouse foreman. Susan studied him for a moment. So this was her adversary. No, she thought, adversary was the wrong word; this man wasn't an enemy, he was merely a chance player in a charade that would be unfolding around him.

She would never meet her real adversary—the drug kingpin in South America who was expecting a shipment of oil field parts stuffed full of U.S. currency and would be arrested upon taking receipt of it. And she would meet his accomplices only briefly—just long enough to help them pack illgotten U.S. dollars into the equipment for the benefit of hidden video cameras. Yet, enemy or pawn, Haggerty could be dangerous to her. Since she would be working with him closely in the coming weeks, he was the person who would have most opportunity to see through her pretense, and she mustn't let him suspect that she was not who she was pretending to be.

As she observed him from afar, Haggerty walked to the coffee maker at one end of the loft landing and paused. Then, as though he sensed that he was being watched, he tilted his head in her direction. Susan quickly averted her gaze and began trodding a meandering path toward the concrete stairs that led to the loft.

Peter's words passed through her mind. "Haggerty's new on the job, and you'll be his supervisor. He'll be as anxious about meeting you as you will about meeting him."

She'd laughed. "Isn't that what they say about rattlesnakes in the wild?"

Susan wasn't laughing now. This undercover assignment was no longer a fantasy adventure, and Clark Haggerty was no longer a flat image on a personnel-file photograph. He was a flesh-and-blood man at the top of the stairs, a man she was going to have to deceive into thinking she was someone else, a woman glamorous and flamboyant and entirely different from Susan Carlson. With each step that brought her closer to Haggerty, she was more firmly convinced that facing a rattlesnake would be less perilous.

From his perch near the coffee maker Haggerty watched Susan zigzag through the maze of crates. So this was Steffie Meeks, Victor Logan's "administrative assistant"—the exotic and beautiful Steffie Meeks, who'd slept her way to the second highest rung on the Logan International executive ladder in a little over two years. She would be his boss until Logan was out of the hospital and able-bodied, which could take months. Haggerty tasted the bile rising in his throat at the prospect of playing yes man to this ambitious finagler. His eyes never left the subject of his gall as he filled his mug and then took a hefty swig of the fresh coffee, letting the hot, dark liquid burn away the lump in his throat. *Easy* he warned himself, *you can't afford to blow this job because of masculine ego.*

Reports of her beauty had not been exaggerated, he thought snidely, as she drew nearer. If Logan had to fool around, he at least had a good eye for the feminine form. Haggerty even felt a lick of compassion for old Victor. He must have been a man in the midst of mid-life crisis when he met Steffie Meeks, and any man developing a paunch and beginning to lose his hair would be vulnerable to flattery from such a striking young woman.

From the distance of half a warehouse, the most noticeable thing about her was the color of her hair, a cross between pink and strawberry blond. The color was striking, daring, a badge of effrontery that seemed to challenge, "This is the way I like it, and I'll not apologize for wearing it." That was consistent with the barracuda image he'd formed of Steffie Meeks based on shop gossip.

Haggerty's second impression was of her size—or, rather, the lack of it. A reputation for reckless ambition had made Logan's mistress sound larger than life, imposing. The woman making her way across the warehouse floor was average in height and compactly built. He had been expecting... he couldn't decide exactly what he'd been expecting. A scarlet letter, perhaps? An *M* for mistress or an *O* for opportunist emblazoned across her chest? At the very least he'd thought she'd be an imposing woman with a tailored-suit corporate bearing, not a petite woman wearing a baby-blue dress with a fluffy bow at the neck.

For Susan, the moment of reckoning had come. The man with whom she must maintain the masquerade was at the top of the stairs. She forced a smile that felt plastic as she stepped onto the bottom step, and kept it plastered on her face as she climbed the stairs. "You must be Haggerty," she said as she reached the landing. "I'm Steffie Meeks, Mr. Logan's assistant. I'll be filling in for him for a few weeks."

"I've been expecting you," he said, accepting the lotion-scented hand she extended. Compared to his it was small and soft, but her grasp was firm. "What's the latest report from the hospital?"

"He's recovering as well as can be expected," she said. "It'll be a long process, but you know Victor—he's strong as an ox and stubborn as a mule, so he'll be up and around in no time."

"Let's hope so." Haggerty looked her straight in the eyes, as he did everyone he met. It was his way of sizing up a person—friend, acquaintance or adversary. Steffie Meeks's eyes were a shocking shade of green, almost as remarkable as the color of her hair. Even more arresting than the color was the tincture of anxiety reflected in the depths of those green eyes. It caught him off guard. He'd been expecting challenge, not timidity. He'd been prepared to dislike

Steffie Meeks for her brashness, but he was totally unprepared to find himself liking her. She was shy, this little lady with a big reputation.

And she'd probably endure torture before she'd let anyone know it. The thought amused him, and he felt a grudging respect for her spunk.

He lingered on her eyes a few seconds too long, and realized with a start that he could get lost in their intriguing depths. He shifted his weight slightly and cleared his throat. This woman was his boss's woman. For the sake of his job, he'd better remember that. He smiled. "Coffee?" he asked. "I was just getting a cup."

"No, thank you," Susan answered with a shake of her head. She wasn't about to add caffeine to the adrenaline already pumping through her system. "I think I'll get after the paperwork that's been piling up on Victor's desk."

Haggerty watched her walk away. The view of this woman was good from any angle. Perhaps working with her wouldn't be as unpleasant as he'd anticipated, as long as he remembered two things: hands off and protect the jugular. Between her looks and her driving ambition, a man could discover he was bleeding to death before he even realized he'd been struck.

Susan sank—and continued sinking—into the seat of the armchair behind Victor Logan's desk, wishing the thick padding could swallow her entirely. She could use a dark, private place to hide while she regained her equilibrium. Though she was certain she'd hidden it well, she had been trembling inside during the encounter with Haggerty.

Some undercover ace, she scolded herself. *What the hell are you doing in this intrigue? You should be back at the bridge making sure no one brings more than his legal quota of liquor back from Mexico.*

The barrier separating Victor Logan's office from Haggerty's was glass from ceiling to midwall, giving her a clear view of Haggerty as he riffled through a stack of papers on his desk. Now she noticed details she had been too preoccupied to see during their brief encounter. The photo in his personnel file had shown him to be a nice-looking man with strong cheekbones and jawline, full lips, thick eyebrows above large, dark eyes. The living, breathing, three-dimensional Clark Haggerty was much more impressive than the flat mug-shot image she had studied all weekend. The photo hadn't shown her the broad shoulders and wide chest, the strong, substantial hands or the aura of competence Clark Haggerty exuded as he worked.

After scrawling a note on the form he was reading, he flipped it face down on a stack of papers to his right and, pausing momentarily in his work, glanced up and caught Susan gaping at him unabashedly.

For an instant they were both frozen by the awkward visual confrontation. Then Haggerty smiled, a self-conscious grin of a smile that seemed to say, "Okay, so you were looking at me. So what?"

Susan smiled back and nodded while she carried on a desperate conversation with herself in her mind. What now? *Do something, dumbbell!*

The dimensions of Victor Logan's desk were approximately those of the state of Rhode Island. Her eyes desperately scanned the wide expanse of veneer and settled on the stacked boxes on the right front corner. The in box was heavily laden with file folders stuffed with white and colored papers. The out box was empty. With an air of what she hoped looked like cool efficiency, she reached for the top folder in the in box. It was filled with the forms Victor Logan had explained to her—pink, blue, yellow, all routine. Reading them should make her look busy enough for an hour or so. She had learned enough about the basic forms to spot any glaring irregularities or conspicuous blanks, and she flagged those forms so that she could discuss them with Victor Logan when she visited him at the hospital.

Ostensibly Logan was in a private room under close medical supervision after suffering a severe heart attack while recuperating from minor surgery. That was the cover story fabricated by the Task Force. The real truth was that Logan had awakened from general anesthesia after undergoing a hemorrhoidectomy, to find his bed surrounded by federal agents dressed in surgical gowns.

The deal they offered him was blunt. They knew he'd been allowing local drug dealers to pack currency in oil field equipment that his firm was shipping to a kingpin in South America. If he cooperated with an international effort to hang the kingpin, he might avert the certain failure of his business and a possible prison sentence.

Word of his grave illness was circulated, along with the information that his administrative assistant, Steffie Meeks, widely known to be his mistress as well as his right hand in the business, would be taking over for him at the Logan International warehouse while he was recuperating.

The real Steffie Meeks was enjoying a vacation on the West Coast under the watchful guard of federal agents, and Susan had stepped into her shoes—or at least leather pumps similar to the ones Steffie usually wore. Susan was an inch shorter than the real Steffie, and her shoe size was a full size smaller than Steffie's. Quite literally, she hadn't been able to fill Steffie's shoes. It had seemed a bad omen when she thought of it that way, but by then it had been too late to back out of the assignment.

Susan finished her survey of the forms and opened the mountain of mail that had accumulated on Logan's desk since his "heart attack." She weeded out solicitations for donations, subscriptions and memberships, leaving perhaps a dozen significant letters for Logan's perusal. She put them, along with the folder of flagged forms, in Steffie's portfolio, then consulted the digital clock on the desk. She'd managed to kill an hour and a half.

Next to the clock was a photo of a chicly dressed woman and two wholesome teenagers. It intrigued her. Mrs. Victor Logan and offspring. The complacent wife content to ignore her husband's blatant affair in order to maintain her social standing as Mrs. Victor Logan, and the kids caught in the middle. What did they think of his philandering, the time he spent with Steffie instead of at home? Did they resent their father? Hate him? Could they respect their mother for her ability to close out the truth, or did they hold her in disdain for her lack of self-respect? Susan sighed softly. What a riddle people made of their lives—Victor Logan by his actions, his wife by her inaction.

Not for the first time, Susan wondered what kind of person Steffie Meeks was, deep down inside. She had seen photos and videos of the woman she was impersonating, and she could see, as Peter had seen, the uncanny similarities between Steffie's face and her own. Yet she knew nothing of this woman she resembled so strikingly. How did Steffie feel about the riddle she was a part of? Did she begrudge her lover his family, her lover's wife the social standing? Did she hope Logan would leave his wife and marry her instead? Did she love him, or was she using him as a shortcut up the corporate ladder and to an oppulent life-style?

Peter had been full of descriptive phrases as he worked on transforming Susan into Steffie: ambitious, shrewd, gutsy, extravagant, self-centered, ruthless, sharp-tongued, quick-witted, fanatically loyal to Logan. Steffie was polite but distant to the secretaries at the corporate offices. She had visited the warehouse infrequently, and rarely spoke to the

laborers there. That aloofness, coupled with the fact
that Haggerty had never met Steffie Meeks, had
made the switch seem viable to the Task Force. The
loading dock workers who'd seen her only from afar
were unlikely to question her identity, and Haggerty
would have no reason to. It was a cinch operation,
even for a cold recruit, as Peter had so often assured
her during her orientation.

Except, of course, that Susan's temperament and
value system were diametrically opposed to Steffie's. Susan was a true democrat, oblivious to caste
systems and corporate pecking orders. Affecting
Steffie Meeks's haughty detachment was going to be
the toughest part of this assignment for her.

Pondering the riddle of Steffie Meeks and Victor
Logan made Susan restless. She walked to the window in the side wall. On the level below, the dock
crew was busily unloading pallets from a truck. As
she watched, she envied them the physical exertion
of the job. Her body was taut as a compressed spring
with anxiety over the charade she had started. Being
able to move around would be cathartic. She settled
for taking a few slow, deep breaths.

Back at Logan's desk, she fished the notes for her
interview with Haggerty from the portfolio. Might as
well get another hurdle behind her. A long, analyti-
cal look at the bank of buttons on the phone en-
abled her to dial Haggerty's desk through the office
intercom. Susan heard his phone ringing and
watched through the glass wall as he answered it. It
struck her as funny that she could hear his voice fil-

ter through the wall as he barked, "Haggerty," into the receiver, and she had to choke down a giggle before she could reply.

"Steffie here," she said, still fighting for control. "Would you mind coming into my office? There are some things we need to go over."

Here goes, she thought as he left his office and his footsteps grated on the concrete surface of the loft floor. Peter's advice had been brief and direct: "You'll be in charge. Act like it." *I'm in charge, I'm in charge, I'm in charge*... The chant echoed in her mind like the locomotive in the kids' storybook saying, "I think I can, I think I can, I think..."

Susan wasn't convinced, but she knew it was unimportant. What was important was that she convince Haggerty, and the cool deference in the tilt of his head as he entered her office and greeted her was reassuring. She was equally cool as she indicated he should sit down in the chair directly opposite her own.

Haggerty sat with his jaw clamped tightly shut and waited to hear why she had formally summoned him to her office. They stared at each other expectantly for a few seconds before Susan shifted in Logan's thronelike chair and said, "How are you faring here at the warehouse, Mr. Haggerty?"

"I haven't noticed any major problem areas," he said evenly.

"Victor—Mr. Logan—was concerned about you being stuck here by yourself before you'd gotten your bearings. He normally spends more time with his new foremen.''

The lines of Haggerty's mouth hardened as he fought off a frown. What point was she trying to make?

She continued. ''Your training seems to have been from the throw-him-in-the-water-and-let-him-sink-or-swim school.'' Her smile was unexpected—and unexpectedly lovely. It overpowered the timidity in her eyes as it reached them, leaving a sparkle that was unclouded.

He smiled back at her without realizing how easily she had penetrated the defenses he'd put up to protect himself from the seduction of her beauty.

''From what I've seen this morning, I'd say you took to the water like a duck,'' she said. ''You're doing a good job, Haggerty.''

He acknowledged the compliment with a nod. Panic gripped Susan's insides. *Here it comes,* she thought, *the part I really have to fake.* Hoping the flush of emotion burning her face wasn't noticeable, she asked, ''Is there anything you'd like to discuss? A particular problem that's cropped up or a question about policy or procedure?''

She waited for his response, fearing he would ask a question Steffie Meeks should be able to answer without batting an eyelash but would leave Susan Carlson sputtering like a blithering idiot. She held her breath. *I'm in charge, I'm in charge, I'm in charge, I'm...*

Haggerty considered the question. "The operations here seem pretty established. I haven't run into any problems..."

Susan slowly exhaled the breath she was holding, then inhaled again sharply.

"...but there are a couple of things you might get better action on than I've been able to manage."

An *I doubt it* crept into the litany of *I'm in charge, I'm in charge...* Susan compelled herself to look directly into his face. "I'll do what I can." She forced what she hoped was a receptive expression on her face.

"There are a couple of things. First, a dock employee named Carlos Gutierrez filed some insurance claims over a month ago, and there's been no action. He came to me about it last week. Apparently he had to pay the medical bills out of his pocket, and it's creating a financial hardship for him. I thought perhaps, since the claims went through the corporate offices, you could find out what's taking so long on this one. I checked the insurance booklet and it says most claims are paid within three weeks."

She exhaled again. This was something she could refer to Logan, and he'd refer it to his secretary. "Of course. I'll check into it. Spell his name for me." It felt good to have something to do as she picked up the pen, even if her fingers were shaky.

To Haggerty, she seemed even smaller than she had earlier. Only the tops of her shoulders and her head were visible from behind Logan's enormous desk. She looked abysmally uncomfortable as she made the notation in her notebook, with her elbows almost level with her shoulders. Even the chair was too big. *Good grief!* he thought exasperatedly. *This woman is acting head of a corporation and she doesn't have the sense to adjust a chair so she can reach the desk.*

The situation seemed so foolish that he didn't know whether to laugh or cry. But he was smart enough to realize that a bit of tact was in order. He cleared his throat, and she tilted her head toward him expectantly. "If you'd like me to raise that chair for you a bit, I'd be happy to," he volunteered.

"My chair?"

"The height adjustment. If we raised it a bit, you could . . . you'd be more comfortable."

"The height adjustment," she echoed. "Of course. I was going to do something about that." He wasn't conned, and she knew it, but it seemed only a minor defensiveness. She stood up and smiled at him sweetly as he walked around the desk. Surely a calculated smile was a universal enough feminine gesture that even Steffie Meeks resorted to one occasionally.

Haggerty's response to the smile was instantaneous and directly sexual and caught him completely off guard. Heaven help him! Why here and this woman? Thank goodness he had caught himself and turned away before she could notice.

"Let's see what we've got here," he said, squatting next to the chair and tilting it so he could see its base. The mechanism worked by lifting a lever and rotating the chair up or down on a thread, then lowering the lever back into position. "It's in the lowest position," he said.

"Victor's a large man."

Haggerty was already spinning the chair up the spindle. "A few inches ought to..." His voice trailed off, leaving the thought unfinished. Beyond the chair, her calves, shapely beneath the billow of the soft skirt of her dress, were at his eye level. They tapered to slender ankles above the graceful elevation of her high-heeled pumps. The discomfort he'd thought was subsiding worsened. Clicking the lever into place, he set the chair upright. "Give it a try," he said, rolling it in her direction, hoping to divert her attention from him as he stood up.

"This is much better. Thank you." Her voice was as warm as a caress, and her perfume, a light blend of floral and musk, played havoc with his senses.

"You're welcome," he grumbled, returning to his own chair, anxious to put as much distance as possible between them. His singular goal was to get out of this office, away from this woman, so he could collect his wits.

Susan drew some confidence from not having to worry about bumping her chin on the desk as she talked, but she sensed that she was *not* in control of the situation. There was a restlessness in Haggerty suddenly, discernible in his inattention. She attacked the situation directly. "What was the other matter you wanted to discuss?"

He jerked to attention. "Other matter?"

"You said there were a couple of things you wanted to discuss. What was there besides Gutierrez's medical claim?"

Haggerty shifted uncomfortably in his chair and admonished himself to concentrate on business as he noticed the way the soft fabric of her dress draped over her breasts. What *was* it he'd wanted to bring up? Oh, yes. The Davis situation. He swallowed the lump in his throat and said, "Brian Davis over at Davis Inc. has been calling me daily about his shipment to Argentina."

Davis Inc. had been on the list of major Logan clients. Susan remembered that Davis manufactured oil field casings, but Argentina didn't ring any bells. Time for a bluff. "What's the hang-up?"

"They're at their credit limit, and they want an extension. I don't have the authority to raise their ceiling."

"Did you send the paperwork over to the corporate offices?" *Please, Lord, let there be paperwork involved.*

"Yes, but Logan's been indisposed, and Davis is pressing for a decision of some sort. And the shipment is taking up half our holding bay. We've got to either ship it or send it back to Davis."

"If you had the authority, what would you do?"

I'd run around this desk and lift you out of that chair and kiss away all that pristine reserve of yours, he thought. He said, "I've looked over their account. It's clean. And payment for this shipment will be due to Davis within ten days of receipt. It's in his contract with the Argentine people. I think Davis is playing straight with us. He'll pay us as soon as his receivables come in. He just doesn't have any reserve. You know how tight cash flow is in the oil patch right now."

Susan nodded and tried to swallow the lump in her throat unobtrusively. *Cash flow in the oil patch?* Jumping frijoles! This must be how Custer felt leading his troops into Little Big Horn.

"I'd raise their ceiling for this shipment," Haggerty continued, "with the understanding that any future shipments would be cash on the line until the account is paid to ten percent below their usual limit."

Out of sheer ignorance of what to say, Susan just stared at him.

"They've been good customers and, if you don't mind my being blunt, with the general slump in oil patch business I don't see how we can afford to cut off an established client who's got a buying customer."

"It's obvious you've given this some thought. Why don't I think about it and give you an answer tomorrow morning?"

"Davis'll call this afternoon. I'll tell him we'll have a decision by noon tomorrow."

"Good," Susan said, feeling as though a ton of concrete had just crumbled away from where it had been perched on her shoulders. Reluctantly she asked if there was anything else he wanted to discuss.

Gratefully Haggerty told her no and waited to be dismissed. He was anxious to get out of this office and away from her. His senses were playing perverse tricks on him in her presence, simply, he was sure, because he didn't want to be attracted to her. He needed to distance himself from her and regain his perspective. Next time he encountered her, forewarned, he'd be in control of his libidinous urges.

"I want to compliment you again on the job you're doing," Susan said.

Haggerty leaned forward slightly as he acknowledged the compliment, impatient for the dismissal he knew was imminent. He didn't know where the absurd idea of kissing his boss's mistress had come from, but he couldn't shake the fantasy from his mind while he was sitting five feet in front of her. His eyes were drawn to the seductive curve of her lips as she poised them to speak, then hesitated. Say it! he urged her mentally. Quit stalling. You've patted me on the back. The meeting's over. Send me back to my own office and tell me to keep up the good work.

The lips on which his attention was focused curved upward into a smile. "I've got good news for you, Haggerty. Lunch is on Logan International today. Unless you have something planned."

He wished he had something planned. Anything—an appointment for a root canal, jury duty, visiting his great-aunt Flora in the nursing home, taking on a group of terrorists—would be safer than going to lunch with this woman. His boss. His boss's mistress.

Clark thought of the sandwich he usually ordered at the supermarket deli a mile up the road. He remembered sleek calves and slender ankles. He remembered that Victor Logan owned Logan International and that Steffie Meeks was Victor Logan's woman. "Lunch sounds great," he said with all the enthusiasm of a drowning man who'd been thrown a bag of rocks.

Chapter Two

Haggerty was in deeper trouble than he thought. He recognized it the moment he closed the door on the passenger side of the Corvette, entombing himself with Steffie in the small space that was permeated by the scent of her perfume. Her hand grazed his hip as she fastened her seat belt, and he responded immediately and intensely to her touch.

Steffie, on the other hand, appeared not even to notice the contact. She seemed, in fact, unaware of his presence as she fiddled with the air-conditioning controls. Finally, with the engine purring evenly and the air conditioner set the way she liked it, she leaned back against the driver's seat and looked at him expectantly.

"Problem?" he asked, after enduring her authoritative look for several awkward seconds.

"Fasten your seat belt."

"My seat belt?"

"It's the law. No use getting a ticket."

The smug righteousness of her attitude stung his ego. "You're the boss," he grumbled, groping for the clasp on the seat belt.

Yes, she thought, amused. When it came to seat belts, she was a tyrant. She'd proved it numerous times with Greg Junior and Kara. And she'd thought she hadn't any background to prepare her for the role of executive!

Haggerty jerked the belt across his lap and shoulders and snapped it in place, being fastidiously careful to avoid any contact with her as he did so.

Susan was oblivious to his caution as she steered the Corvette out of the parking lot, concentrating on the route she'd memorized to Shanghai Red's. Peter had insisted Susan follow Steffie's established pattern of expense-account lunches at popular restaurants. He'd suggested Shanghai Red's, which was close to the warehouse and flashy enough for Steffie's flamboyant taste, but a place where Steffie wasn't particularly well known.

Feeling like the country mouse who'd just wandered into the glow of big-city lights, Susan had to police herself to keep from goggling over the sprawling seafood restaurant that was decorated in the motif of a waterfront warehouse. Outside the glass wall next to their table a tugboat chugged past unhurriedly on a finger of the ship channel, and the weathered dinginess of the tugboat lent its lazy voyage a sense of poetry.

While Susan watched the drama outside the window, Haggerty watched Susan, his eyes drawn to her beauty. The peculiar pinkish-auburn of her hair turned her fair skin into bisque, and the jarring green of her eyes glowed with a light of wonderment as she drank in the nautical drama outside.

"Do you come here often?" he asked.

She blinked those remarkably green eyes and then focused them on his face as though she'd forgotten his existence. "Not as often as I'd like."

It was, perhaps, the first totally truthful statement she'd made all day, and Clark heard the intensity in the timbre of her voice and saw it in the depths of her eyes and wondered why a view from a restaurant window dazzled her so.

He decided it must be that Logan couldn't afford to be seen with her in public too often. Their affair was general knowledge at Logan International, but Logan could hardly flaunt his relationship with her on his wife's time. Probably an occasional lunch was all he could risk without compromising his wife's credibility with the socialites she worked with on various charitable projects. The "right people" would be willing to overlook a few "business" lunches, but not a blatant public courtship between a married man and his mistress.

For the first time, Haggerty wondered why Steffie Meeks was willing to settle for a role as mistress, even one that came with a shortcut up the corporate ladder. It was a riddle he would ponder repeatedly in the coming weeks. The obvious answer, that Steffie probably put up with being Logan's mistress because she was in love with Logan, worried at him like an overstarched collar.

The serene tattoo of the water's gentle splash against the bank, and the sluggish pace of the tugboat's unhurried passage, were soothing to Susan's shattered nervous system, and she was beginning to feel, if not relaxed, at least comfortable in the role of Steffie Meeks. That her audience of one seemed to accept her identity without suspicion was reassuring enough to renew her confidence in her ability to do the job she had undertaken.

All morning she had been too preoccupied with convincing Haggerty that she was Steffie Meeks to relate to him on a personal level. Now, from across the narrow table, she considered the man with whom she was having lunch.

Haggerty's chambray warehouse shirt with a logo patch above one breast pocket and his name appliquéd in script above the other should have made him seem out of place in the midday crowd of businessmen and women, yet it didn't. His square face, wide jaw, full cheekbones and classic features were tempered into rugged handsomeness by the fine web of lines radiating from his eyes, and a faint triangular scar on his right cheek contributed just the right aura of macho mystique. There was an unapologetic earthiness about him that said, "I am what I am, and I'm comfortable with it. You can be, too."

He caught her looking at him and smiled. Susan was fishing for a suitable conversation opener when she became aware of a sensual smolder in the depths of his milk-chocolate-brown eyes. Blatantly masculine and frankly sexual, it roused an awareness in her that she thought had atrophied when Greg had died. From her prickling scalp to her tingling toes, the fact that she was a woman registered on nerve endings, paralyzing her lungs in their routine quest for breath and sucking the moisture from her throat. She worried that the heat stabbing through her might be visible in the form of a blush rising under her sheer foundation makeup.

Unwittingly, through the simple fact of his virility, this man was reminding her that she was a woman, alive with human needs that until now she had been suppressing. Consciously she fought the sudden, alarming awareness that the male glint in his eye had prodded into full wakefulness. Her instinct was the most basic response to fear—flight.

Abruptly she excused herself and found her way to the ladies' room. Trembling, she leaned against the cold, uncomforting wall and wondered what was happening to her. She felt like a small lost child, far away from home and abysmally alone and vulnerable. Why this resurrection of sexual awareness now when she had to concentrate on the job she was doing? Why not months—a year—ago when she had begun lying awake nights wondering why she couldn't feel normal urges toward the men who flirted with her? Why not with Tyler Fannin—solid citizen, well-heeled Tyler Fannin, her friend since childhood who wanted her to marry him?

She fought a wave of nausea in her throat. Oh, God, why with this man, the last man in the world who should make her feel this way? *What was she doing here, playing undercover cop? Why wasn't she back in Brownsville with her children and her perfectly routine job where she belonged?*

Her mother had tried to warn her she wasn't sophisticated enough for such intrigue, but Susan hadn't listened. She was, after all, an adult, capable of recognizing her own abilities and limitations, and she felt she could handle the assignment Peter had offered her. Appalled that her mother could doubt her capabilities and her judgment, Susan, still stinging at the betrayal, had nevertheless clenched her jaw against bitter rejoinders and proceeded with arrangements for her trip to Houston in a silent, dramatic display of rebellion that made not marrying Tyler Fannin pale, in her mother's eyes, from a felony into a minor misdemeanor.

Creeping cautiously out of the stall and finding herself alone, she wet a paper towel at the sink and pressed it to her face, unmindful of the makeup she had laboriously applied that morning, and heaved a long, soulful sigh. Her mother had been right; it had been a mistake to come here. If a simple glint in a man's eye could send her cowering to the ladies' room, she *wasn't* sophisticated enough to play a worldly lady executive involved in a high-profile love affair.

The sigh had drained her. Now she felt strangely as though she were filling up again. With what, she couldn't define. Resolve? Confidence? A grave acceptance of the inevitability of having to finish a job she'd started? After another swipe of the damp towel, she blended away the streaks in her makeup and reluctantly abandoned the safety of the powder room.

Haggerty was still shell-shocked when he spied her returning. He knew what he had seen, but logic told him it couldn't have happened. One fleeting second of intense communication—a shared knowledge of a natural force working between them—and Steffie had taken off looking like a terrified ingenue in a monster flick.

Instinctively Haggerty knew it was not just his unguarded revelation of sexual interest that had sent her flying. He'd seen the flash of response in her eyes, the rising color in her face before she'd fled. She'd been running from herself as well as from the monster. It was the sort of reaction one would expect from a schoolgirl caught flirting with one boy when she's going steady with another, not from a woman like Steffie Meeks. She couldn't consider one innocuous flicker of sexual interest a serious infidelity to a married lover.

He stood up and pulled out the chair for her when she reached the table, then settled back into his own chair. The waiter had brought their order. Spreading her napkin in her lap, Steffie said, "I'm sorry for making you wait."

He noticed that she didn't look directly at him as she spoke. "No problem," he said. "It just got here."

Susan survived the meal. That's the way she would remember it: survival in the face of crisis. A crisis of confidence, of conviction, of control. Above all, of control. Because no matter how strenuously she avoided eye contact with him, no matter how much distance she put between them by affecting Steffie Meeks's characteristic aloofness, she was now dealing with her awareness of Clark Haggerty's virility and her basic response to that maleness. He was no longer just the LIFT foreman she had to fool. He was a man with the ability to make her face the fact of her own womanhood, something she'd been hiding from for nearly two years. Suddenly she was, as her father would say, playing in a new ballpark.

She felt as though she'd just made a foolish giant leap from a neighborhood sandlot to the world-famous Astrodome, without any preparation for the big leagues.

Chapter Three

Miss Meeks. I was hoping I would run into you. I need to talk with you a moment."

Susan reflected that Peter Warshauer would look like a teddy bear in anything he wore, and that that quality of benign innocence probably served him well in the business of being a federal agent. Today he was wearing surgical scrubs.

"Dr. Peters," she replied, shaking his hand as though this were the chance meeting it was meant to appear. "Of course I have a moment."

She followed him to an open hospital waiting room and took a seat beside him on an abjectly uncomfortable plastic-upholstered couch. His brief survey of the area to ascertain that they wouldn't be overheard was subtle but thorough. He took a deep breath. "Well, Miss Meeks, how was your day?"

"Exhausting," she said. "Undercover work is wearing on the nerves."

"First-day jitters," he said. "You can soak out the kinks in the hot tub tonight. One of the perks on this particular job."

"I'm too tired to count blessings *or* perks tonight."

Peter had had enough small talk. "Start with Haggerty," he said in his crisp, professional agent voice.

Haggerty. Susan exhaled a soft, weary sigh. "What do you want to know?"

"You met him? How was it?"

"No problems," she said, thinking, *Unless you count the fact that he's the first man I've been strongly attracted to since my husband died.* Forcing her mind back to business, she continued, "He seemed absorbed in running the warehouse. I don't think he questioned who I was at all."

"Good," Peter said. "How about the work itself?"

"I have a few things to go over with Logan, but nothing tripped me up. I guess I faked it pretty well."

Peter, accustomed to reading people, picked up on her ambivalence immediately. "You don't sound exactly proud of yourself," he said.

Susan sighed again. "I just…" She looked straight into the blue slate of his expressionless eyes. "I felt like a liar. I wasn't expecting to feel dishonest."

He patted her hand in what would appear to be a normal comforting gesture from a doctor discussing a patient. "Occupational hazard," he said. "You'll get over it as you get farther into the job."

"I've heard lying gets easier with practice," she said waspishly.

"You do what you have to do..."

"...to get the job done," Susan finished for him. How many times had he told her that during her whirlwind orientation? He'd said it while the hair-stylist was cropping seven inches from her hair to create layered bangs and repeated it while the color consultant applied the grotesque-colored gel that would achieve apricot fizz. "I'll get it done, Peter, but I don't have to like it."

He patted her hand again. "Like it or not, the job's perking. And it's time for the devoted Steffie Meeks to visit her ailing lover."

"I can hardly wait."

Just outside the door to Logan's private room, Peter leaned over and whispered in Susan's ear. "Don't get him too stirred up. He's supposed to be a sick man."

Susan rewarded him with a crooked grin of exasperation. Peter could be obnoxious and tunnel-visioned, but his wry wit was a redeeming quality.

It was almost eight o'clock when Susan reached Steffie's condo, and she decided to do her soaking in the sunken whirlpool tub in the bathroom instead of at the public hot tub in the amenities area. It had

been a long day as well as an eventful and emotion-
ally taxing one, and she preferred to de-kink her
kinks without an audience of fellow de-kinkers.

With soft music playing in the background, a
profusion of tropical plants flourishing under the
skylight and several scented candles flickering in
front of the mirrored wall opposite the tub, Steffie's
luxurious garden bath was a more than adequate
setting for unwinding. And thinking. And not
thinking. Susan alternated between the two, relaxing her neck against the back of the tub while the
warm water swirled around her and random thoughts
about her first day as Steffie Meeks swirled through
her mind.

Inevitably she found herself pondering the specter of Clark Haggerty, remembering too well the
flicker of sexual interest in his eyes and the startling
lightning bolt of response that had shot through her
when she'd recognized it. She'd overreacted, of
course, dashing off to the ladies' room like a scared
rabbit darting down a hole.

The idea of a rabbit running away from a sensual
leer struck her as preposterous, and she giggled.
Everyone knew where rabbits stood on the subject,
and practice, of sex. The giggle faded as she let her
shoulders sink a bit deeper into the water. She was no
rabbit; she was a woman, and her renegade sexual
attraction to Clark Haggerty posed a complex problem. She was going to be spending a lot of time with
Haggerty for two, possibly three, weeks, and she was

going to have to put a lid on any emotional involvement with him before it had a chance to run amok.

The sound of her ragged sigh was lost in the whoosh and gurgle of the churning water. Of all the possible complications she might have anticipated with this assignment, developing a hankering for Clark Haggerty would have been on the bottom of her list—if she'd even thought to include it. In the two years since Greg's death, she hadn't enjoyed what the women's magazines would consider a scintillating love life. It had taken several months just to feel comfortable going out anywhere with friends, and several months more before she could bring herself to accept a solo "date" with Tyler, whom she'd known all her life.

Tyler, her mother's best friend's son, was the older brother Susan had adopted to help her through the woes and trials of adolescence. Ever the faithful friend, he had been on the scene to console her immediately after Greg's death. Susan didn't doubt that she loved Tyler, but her feelings toward him were fraternal, not romantic.

Tyler's feelings were another matter. Recently he'd indicated that he would like to move their relationship to a new plane. He wanted to get married and, as he put it, "legitimize the relationship," which to date had been platonic. Susan had been hedging. She was comfortable with Tyler as a friend, but she felt no desire to take on Tyler as a formal suitor. And though he seemed to be drawing from an inexhaustible font of patience in waiting for her to make some commitment, Susan knew she had to come to some decision about the status of their relationship soon. It was unfair to keep Tyler's life on hold indefinitely.

Susan's mother's advice had been simple and straightforward: Marry the man. As heir to the town's largest independent furniture store, he could offer Greg Junior and Kara a prosperity Susan's job at the border station couldn't.

"And he adores you, Susan," Louise Owens had told her daughter. "He's always adored you. The way he used to look at you when you were a teenager! He was just waiting for you to grow up so he could marry you. Then you threw a wrench in the works by meeting Greg."

A native Pennsylvanian, Greg had been transferred to Brownsville by a national car-rental chain when, according to Louise Owens, local boys could have used the job. Louise had never quite forgiven her daughter for falling in love with an outsider. Begrudgingly she had admitted that Greg was goodlooking, hardworking and loyal, and she had warmed to him when she'd seen what a doting father he was to her grandchildren, but she'd never really accepted him as family the way she had anticipated accepting Lorna Fannin's boy, Tyler.

In Louise's mind, Tyler Fannin was the perfect match for her daughter; Greg Carlson, despite his charm, had been a carpetbagger. Louise regretted Greg's tragic death and the heartbreak it had caused her daughter and grandchildren, but she was a practical woman. Greg Carlson was dead, and no one could do anything about it, but Tyler Fannin was alive and interested in Susan, and Louise wasn't going to let her daughter pass up a good thing twice. This time she wasn't pussyfooting around, mincing words about what an eligible, suitable man Tyler was.

Susan was torn between duty to her mother and children and duty to her happiness, between the logic of marrying Tyler and the folly of waiting for another charming prince to ride into her life the way Greg had. Greg had been crepe suzettes and champagne; Tyler was pot roast and iced tea. She'd had her crepes and champagne; perhaps now she should listen to her mother and settle for the pot roast. But something in her rebelled against settling for less than she wanted in a relationship that should be spiced with romance as well as respect. An innate sense of fair play told her she would be cheating Tyler and herself.

There were times when Susan resented the dilemma Tyler presented in her life, and wondered why marriage had to be an issue at all. Thanks to Greg's life insurance and her job on the bridge, she wasn't destitute. And two kids were enough to fill anyone's life with love. So why the big rush to get her to the altar? Why did she have to have a man—any man— in her life, if she couldn't have a man who could make her feel the way Greg had made her feel?

"Because you're not eighteen anymore, the way you were when you met Greg," Louise had told her.

"You're a woman now. You can't expect to go to the circus without smelling the elephants."

The timer on the whirlpool shut off, and the thrashing water sucked to a halt. Susan stepped out of the tub, then dried off in one of Steffie's velour bath blankets. A towel for two? she thought, hanging it on the bar to dry. For when Victor Logan slipped away from home long enough for a rendezvous in the tub?

Obviously Steffie Meeks valued the zing of romance, even if she found it with another woman's husband. Susan looked at the sunken oval tub, empty except for a froth of bubbles next to the drain, and tried to imagine Tyler sitting in it, waiting for her to join him. She couldn't decide whether it was the fantasy or the cold air pumping through the air-conditioning vent above her that made her suddenly cold. She just knew, as she wrapped the bath blanket a bit closer around her, that it would be wrong to tie herself to a man when the idea of taking a bath with him left her unaffected.

"You want it all," her mother kept telling her. Susan directed an inquisitional look at the pink-haired stranger in the mirror and remembered the heat that had coursed through her when she'd looked into Clark Haggerty's eyes and realized he appreciated her as a woman.

"Yes," she said aloud. She wanted it all. She wanted zing and fireworks and champagne with a good, steady man. A man who could look at her the way Clark Haggerty had looked at her and make her feel the way she'd felt.

Not Haggerty per se, of course. Any involvement with him was out of the question, though she owed him a debt of gratitude. The excitement he had stirred in her, a fire in the blood, had helped bring into focus her objections to settling for a near-fraternal relationship with Tyler. The sad truth was that Susan had begun to doubt she could experience that fire in the blood. She'd begun to believe that the part of her that allowed her to feel it had been born when she'd met Greg and had died inside her when she'd buried him. Now she knew that that part of her wasn't dead. If she felt the fire with Haggerty, she could feel it again someday with the right man.

She'd handle Clark Haggerty, as Peter would say, because Clark Haggerty would have to be handled. But eventually another man would light that special fire—a man who didn't have to be handled. And Susan would be waiting.

Susan decided to handle the issue of Clark Haggerty by ignoring the fact that Clark was an issue. Her attraction to him wouldn't come as a surprise anymore, and forewarned was forearmed. She would be prepared for her feelings and able to control them. Once she had given it some thought, she'd realized Haggerty shouldn't present too much of a problem anyway. He was in a more precarious situation than she was. So long as he remained convinced that she was Steffie Meeks, she was safe, because he could hardly afford to try to seduce his boss's mistress.

While Susan was pondering the problem of Clark Haggerty, Haggerty was pondering the dilemma posed by his attraction to Ms. Steffie Meeks. Just as he'd been drawn to her all day, his mind was obsessed with her all evening, putting him in a foul mood. He didn't need any complications on the job he'd just started, and he certainly hadn't anticipated this one. He was just going to have to get his act together where she was concerned. There was a future to this job, and he wasn't going to let some adolescent reaction to a pair of sexy green eyes and chorus-line legs jeopardize that future.

The next morning Susan and Clark drove to the warehouse in separate vehicles from opposite directions, each brimming with resolve to do his or her respective job without any interference from sexual chemistry.

It worked for a while. They managed to maintain an attitude of cool courtesy, exchanging small talk at the coffee maker or watercooler and nodding when they chanced to catch each other's eye through the glass wall separating their offices.

By midday, Susan was burning with the realization that the stab of sexual excitement she'd felt at the restaurant was no simple fluttering of the hormones brought on by her anxiety over the masquerade. It was a bona fide reaction to Clark Haggerty. The rugged beauty of his face, the breadth of his shoulders, the masculine gait of his walk fascinated her. And the desire she'd seen in his eyes was still there, still smoldering in their brown depths. He was as aware of her as a woman as she was of him as a man. It thrilled her. It scared her. It made her feel as though her womanhood were being drawn back to life after a long period of banishment.

They became engaged in the perpetual game of cat and mouse, playing a kind of erotic peekaboo, stealing glances at each other, catching each other stealing glances, pretending they didn't notice what was going on between them. Polite greetings and small talk were lines in a farce they were acting out. Always there was an undercurrent of awareness between them, despite their attempts at detachment. Susan fought the undertow by retreating into Steffie Meeks's haughty aloofness; Clark's response was brusqueness that bordered on hostility.

Neither of them was fooled. They were jesters in the court of romance, dancing to a music as old as mankind. Neither misread a line from the farce on Tuesday, and each left the warehouse filled with a sense of reprieve. From what, neither knew.

They survived Wednesday and endured Thursday and arrived for work on Friday filled with fresh stores of resolve to tackle their jobs without missing a cue in the farce or a step in the dance. Neither of them could afford a mistake. Romance was an unforgiving king, known to destroy the reason of jesters who made mistakes in the prescribed rituals of his court. Susan and Clark each had valid reasons for not wanting to lose the power of reason. Each had a job to do that could be imperiled by a foolish mistake.

Friday afternoon, Susan stood at the window overlooking the loading dock and watched Clark operating the forklift. The machine moved smoothly under his control, attesting to his skill as an operator. He was that type of man, she thought. The type of man who'd know how to do any job in the warehouse before he'd expect others to work there under his authority. A hands-on supervisor, the classified ads would call him.

Hands on. Was that ever a loaded phrase—a phrase to conjure up fantasies in the mind of a frustrated woman. He had nice hands; she had become fascinated with them the morning before. They were beautiful in a masculine way, large, strong, mannishly rough. A warmth began somewhere in her middle and spread through her body, bringing a blush to her face. Clark Haggerty was a hands-on man; she was imagining what it would be like for him to have his hands on her.

With a heavy sigh, she went back to her desk and looked for something to divert her attention from the man downstairs. For half a minute she propped her elbows on the desk and buried her still-flushed face in her hands, wondering for the umpteenth time what she was going here. Greg Junior had a cold and had sounded pitiful when he'd told her how much he missed her, and Kara had been chosen for a part in a PTO program that Mother couldn't attend because she was away playing undercover agent. So while

Susan knew she should properly be coddling her sick son and oohing over her daughter's dramatic debut, she was fantasizing about being touched by a man who didn't even know her proper name.

A fine mess you've gotten yourself into, she thought in disgust. *You're a lousy absentee mother because you're playing agent, and you're a lousy agent because you're letting your glands get in the way.*

One thing this assignment had taught her was that looking busy was more demanding and often more exhausting than actually being busy. She reviewed the paperwork on every shipment into the warehouse, alert for one destined to a certain corporation in Colombia. When it arrived, she would notify the kingpin's local errand boy, and a time would be set up for loading the currency. The products to be "loaded"—usually casing or pipe joints—never came from the same company, which is why it had taken the Task Force so long to zero in on Logan International's role in the smuggling operation. In fact, the operation was so nebulous that even Victor Logan didn't know in advance where the shipments would originate. They simply came in about once a month, Logan phoned his contact, the currency was loaded and the product was shipped.

So far, nothing significant had passed her desk, and Susan was stuck with the chore of finding something to fill her time at the office. Today, as she sifted through the papers a second time in hope of finding something that demanded her attention, she discovered a discrepancy between a bill of lading and a customs declaration form, the result of a careless clerical error by the corporate office staff. The customs forms should be retyped with the proper information.

Unable to locate a stash of blank forms in Logan's files, she went to the storage room on the edge of the loft beyond Haggerty's office. It was a long, narrow room with metal shelves against each wall, and the shelves were lined with the myriad forms required by the customs agencies of countries throughout the world. The various shapes and colors of the forms, arranged in alphabetical order according to the country requiring them, created an irregular, angular rainbow on the shelves.

Susan ran a polished nail along the labels on the side of the shelves, searching for the one that would identify the customs declaration form she was seeking, and discovered it was stacked on the highest shelf. Standing on tiptoe with her arm extended, she willed herself to reach the form, but the stack remained, perversely, an inch beyond her fingertip. She tried hopping and succeeded only in feeling like an ill-coordinated kangaroo. She could touch the stack, but she couldn't get a grip on one of the forms.

The only thing remotely resembling a step stool in the storage room was an old stenographer's chair in the corner. She wheeled it in front of the shelf, took off her shoes and cautiously mounted the seat of the chair. After a few seconds she adapted to the precarious tilting and bobbing of the chair and made short order of picking up the form.

She was absorbed in checking the number on the top to be sure it was the form she wanted when the sound of her name spoken by Clark's voice startled her. She jumped just enough to set the chair pitching back and forth and had to bend her knees and spread her arms to catch her balance.

After stabilizing herself, she cast a rather severe accusatory look at Clark, who withered not at all under the scowl.

"Careful," he said, "you could break your neck standing on a chair like that." The statement was accompanied by the most natural gesture in the world: he raised his hands as he might to a child stranded in a tree. Susan leaned forward, letting his hands slide under her arms as she stepped off the chair.

Later, as they regretted what happened next, both would reflect that the touch was their undoing.

If only he hadn't touched me...

If only I hadn't touched her...

But Clark had touched her, and he knew he was lost as he looked into the fathomless depths of those brilliant green eyes. All the desire he'd been suppressing exploded with an urgency that terrified him as the floral-tinged musk of her perfume assailed his nostrils. All the frustration over the way he felt about her, all the confusion over why he felt this way about *this* woman, was lost in the overpowering urge to gather her into his arms and crush her against him

and consume the sweetness promised by the voluptuous curve of her lips.

The moment of choice had come: either he
dropped his hands and relinquished his touch on her,
or he succumbed to his need to hold her. There was
no choice, really. A groan of frustration hissed
through his lips as his arms slid around her, and the
last shred of reason flew from his mind with the ra-
tionalization, *It's only a job* ...

The logic that should have warned Susan to stop
what was happening abandoned her as his face
moved toward hers slowly and inevitably. His lips
hovered above hers, hesitating one, perhaps two an-
ticipation-filled seconds. It was not a groan that escaped Susan's lips but a sigh, in that instant before
his mouth reached hers to meld separate fantasies
into a singular reality.

Susan drifted in a world of sensations long forgotten but now stunningly real. Sweetness, fire, excitement filled her, arousing and soothing, igniting
and quenching, slaking and inciting. It wasn't until
she awoke from a magical, mellow oblivion to discover her cheek nestled against his chest and her
arms encircling his waist that the implications of
what she had allowed—encouraged—to happen
closed in on her. How could she have been so careless, so foolish?

Panic stabbed through her, and her mind raced
with questions. What could she do to undo what was
done? How could she salvage her act? In desperation she looked to the character she was portraying

for answers. *What would Steffie do? Say?* Steffie would know how to regain control of the situation; she must think the way Steffie would think.

And plunge knives into hearts in the process.

She drew a deep, fortifying breath before pulling away from the comfortable haven of his arms, straightening her dress with an air of nonchalance and saying, "I guess Victor's been sick longer than I realized."

Chapter Four

The verbal barb landed on target. A punch in the guts would have been gentler; Clark might at least have seen a physical blow coming and been prepared for it.

Stunned, furious, he glowered at Susan, his nostrils flaring, his hands curling into fists, flicking open and curling again as he fought for control over the anger that was consuming him. "Do you expect me to believe I was just a stand-in for Victor Logan?"

Susan didn't want to look at him, to face the fury she had deliberately provoked in him. She didn't want to "handle" Clark Haggerty as though he were simply a complication in an important job. For a few, fleeting moments she had related to him on a human level, and the result had been a rare ecstasy.

She sighed silently and steeled herself for his counterattack, jutting her chin defiantly. She was a woman with a job to do, no matter how much she wished to be simply a woman.

The laugh she forced was bitter and harsh. "Men!" she said. "You kiss the most convenient woman around and expect her to swoon over the honor of having been chosen."

Of all the smart-mouthed, high-handed females, Clark thought. A muscle worked in his otherwise granite jaw, and his nostrils flared again as belligerent gaze met defiant glare.

He'd never wanted a woman so much in his life; the fact that he wanted her—and knew he couldn't have her—fueled a rage that was already a roaring flame. Of their own volition his hands closed around her upper arms, and he shoved his face an inch from hers. "Convenient? Hell, yes, you're convenient, parading around this warehouse in dresses that swish when you walk and wearing that damned perfume." The vulnerability in her eyes should have stopped him, but the emotion she stirred in him was so powerful that he was out of control. "You want convenient? I'll give you convenient."

The contrast between the two kisses was staggering: the first, tender, warm and gentle; the second, rough, urgent and passionate. Susan stood, dumbstruck, her chest heaving as she took in deep gulps of air when he released her. How could the simple act of placing two pairs of lips together be so diverse in execution, so different in effect?

"Nothing personal, you understand, Miss Meeks," Clark said, "just a healthy male and a healthy female taking advantage of a convenient situation." He was halfway through the doorway before she said his name. He turned, ready to spar with her, but his heart softened to mush at the sight of her—small, vulnerable, her lips still bruised by the kiss he'd inflicted on her.

An apology formed in his throat, but he couldn't voice it. Their eyes locked in mutual discomfort and regret. When he finally moved, it was to approach the shelf and take down another copy of the form she held crushed in her hand. "I believe this is the one you wanted."

There was a lump of warm wax where Susan's voice box should have been. She tried to say thank you, but the words simply wouldn't come out, so she nodded mutely and watched him walk away.

The expression on Peter's face would have done credit to a man just informed his wife was keeping company with the Navy's Fifth Fleet. He extended a four-letter barnyard obscenity into three syllables, Texas style. "How in the hell could you have let it happen?"

Susan sat in the hot tub, studying the bubbles frothing from the spigots with great concentration. "I didn't *let* it happen," she said. "It just . . . happened." She looked up into the scowl on Peter's face. "I handled it."

"Are you sure?"

Susan's attention went back to the bubbles; her voice was peculiarly expressionless. "He's more convinced than ever that I'm Steffie Meeks."

"You're not getting hung up on him, are you?"

"I'm not stupid, Peter," she said irritably, then added morosely, "just human."

Peter repeated the obscenity he'd said earlier, this time muttering it under his breath. "This is a fine kettle of fish, Susan. A hell of a note. Working with rookies is a crapshoot at best, but I didn't expect this kind of complication with you, of all people."

"What's that supposed to mean?" Susan demanded.

"It wasn't a slam, Susan. I'm sorry if it sounded that way. But guys talk, you know, men who've seen you at the bridge, and you don't exactly have the reputation of a swinger."

The day had deteriorated from confusing and exasperating to downright awful. "I guess you didn't expect a cold fish from Brownsville to arouse any passions," she said angrily. "I didn't plan for it to happen, Peter. It's not as though I teased Clark Haggerty into kissing me in some grand conspiracy to make your life difficult. This turn of events didn't exactly thrill *me* either."

"Are you quite sure of that?" he asked wryly.

"Bad choice of words," she said. "And whether or not it thrilled me is none of your business."

"You handled it, huh?" Peter asked.

Susan said testily, "Either you trust my judgment or you don't, Peter. I told you I handled it, and I did."

"Well, don't be too conspicuous about turning around, Double-O-Seven, but you're about to have to handle it again."

Very slowly she twisted her head in the direction of his almost imperceptible nod. Clark Haggerty had just entered the amenities area and was approaching the hot tub. She milked Peter's pet obscenity to its full potential.

Chuckling, Peter said, "If you soak much longer, you're going to shrivel up. Break a leg, sweetheart."

"Sadist," Susan snapped as she stood up to get out of the spa.

Clark almost wished he hadn't spied the back of Steffie's head, so recognizable because of the color of her hair, on his way to the stairs that led to her apartment. She was wearing a fluorescent green tanksuit that rode high on her thighs and scooped low enough to reveal the tops of firm, full breasts. His response to the sight of her was immediate and acute. Frowning at his peculiar vulnerability to her, he wondered why he was surprised. His reactions to this woman were too consistent to surprise him anymore. Given a few thousand years alone with her on a desert island, he might be able to satiate this hunger he had for her.

Damn her! He couldn't take his eyes off her as she patted her skin dry with a thick towel. The coverup she put on afterward, a white lace affair, hid little and enticed a lot as it settled over the contrast between bright green cloth and bare flesh. Clark took a deep breath. What was he doing here?

Susan had studiously ignored Clark as she dried off, and didn't acknowledge his presence until they came nose to nose on the sidewalk. "Clark?" she said, feigning surprise.

After an awkward hesitation he said, "I hope you don't mind...I..." He shifted uncomfortably, frowning, and finally added, "I wanted to clear the air between us."

Concentrating on the videos she'd seen of Steffie Meeks, Susan shrugged her shoulders haughtily, as though what Clark Haggerty wanted was of small consequence to her, and said with an offhand brusqueness, "The air, as you call it, did get a bit steamy, didn't it?"

She walked past him, and, uninvited, he fell into step behind her. "Shall we talk here?" he said, indicating a grouping of lawn chairs on a redwood deck.

"I don't like sitting around in a wet suit," she said. The wetness of the suit didn't concern her as much as what it left exposed. Though Susan had purchased it, the suit shouted the infamous Ms. Meeks's taste for flash and flair. Susan knew it flattered her, but she would never have chosen it if she hadn't been trying deliberately to look like Steffie. It wasn't the type of suit a widowed mother wore to the neighborhood pool in a small town, and it certainly wasn't what she wanted to wear while "handling" Clark

Haggerty. Her flesh was already sizzling from the way he kept looking at her. He hadn't missed a single clinging curve of the cloth or a square inch of exposed flesh in his perusal.

Inside the condo, Susan tilted her head toward the bar. "Help yourself to something wet, if you'd like, and make yourself at home. I won't be long."

You're wet, thought Clark. *I'd like to help myself to you.* She had disappeared into a hallway before he could even nod a reply to her invitation. Not even the ice in the drink he mixed could cool down the memory of Steffie in the clinging swimsuit.

Susan purposely took her time showering, shampooing and towel-drying her hair, then applied fresh makeup. She needed time to think about the best way to deal with Haggerty. She was more than ever aware how ill-prepared she was for the operation she'd become involved in so blithely. She was playing by ear on this one because there was no music to read, and her only guide was her ability to put herself inside the mind of a woman she'd never met and try to react the way that stranger would react.

Powdered with Steffie's trademark scent, she rummaged through Steffie's walk-in closet and tried to decide what Steffie would wear. She finally chose a flowing caftan with large salmon-colored fantasy flowers and deep green fern fronds silk-screened on a chartreuse background.

Shoes! she thought, panicking. Her scruffies would never do, and black leather pumps were hardly appropriate. She would have to make do with a pair of Steffie's and hope they didn't fall off. She was in luck. The third shoe box she opened contained a pair of sandals trimmed with salmon and green beads. Though the stationary front straps gaped across her instep, the long back straps, string thin, were made to lace around the ankle and tie into a bow. She couldn't walk a marathon in them, but they would suffice for the living room.

In the hall she uttered the litany to herself: *I'm Steffie Meeks, and I'm in charge. I'm Steffie Meeks and...*

Haggerty stood when she entered the room and sat down again when she settled on the love seat perpendicular to his chair.

"I see you found your way around the bar," she said, nodding toward the frosted glass sweating onto a black-lacquered coaster on the coffee table.

He nodded. "I would have mixed one for you, but I didn't know what you drink."

"White wine," she said, "but I had a glass in the hot tub. I'm not thirsty just now."

The awkwardness between them was almost a tangible thing, and Susan felt almost as much compassion for him as she felt apprehension over having to deal with him. He was obviously uncomfortable, and his confidence, which she suspected was usually unflappable, was now visibly shaken. She found such vulnerability in a large, strong man intriguing. And ingratiating. It was a reminder that, while she was "handling" a problem in a complex operation, she nevertheless was dealing with a human being with a gamut of human strengths and weaknesses—and feelings that could be hurt.

The chemistry between her and Clark was dangerous from her viewpoint because it complicated more than just a relationship. But, she realized, the situation must be just as vexing from Clark's viewpoint. He might be just an innocent bystander in a situation more complex than he realized, but surely he was aware that his bread and butter could be on the line if he got involved with his boss's mistress.

Oh, Cupid, what barbed arrows you fling, Susan thought. *And how haphazardly you aim them.* Her gentle sigh seemed amplified in the strained silence. She wanted to say something, and she thought that probably Clark did, too, but neither of them knew how to begin.

Clark leaned forward, propped his elbows on his knees and blew a puff of air through his steepled fingertips. God, he was a magnificent man, Susan thought. He had the profile of a Roman warrior, with distinct, rugged features. She wondered how he got the scar under his eye.

"We have to talk about this afternoon," he said abruptly, straightening.

Although her job at the border station had toughened her somewhat, Susan was, by nature and practice, a nurturer, given to kissing scraped fingers and hugging away broken hearts and shattered illusions. Deliberately inflicting pain—physical or emotional—went against her grain. As noble as her motivations were, it was difficult for her to affect callousness and batter Clark's ego. But batter it she must. Anger would build a wall between them.

"You're making a mountain out of a molehill, Haggerty. You're a man, I'm a woman, and we've been cooped up together at that warehouse all week."

"It wasn't Mount Everest, Steffie, but it was sure as hell bigger than any molehill to me. And unless my sensors are malfunctioning, it was to you, too."

"Leave it alone, Haggerty. Forget it happened. I intend to."

"And cows fly."

She sniffed in exasperation and forced a note of sarcasm into her voice. "The trouble with big, strong men is the big, strong egos that go along with them. What's wrong, Haggerty? Have a problem with the idea that kissing you isn't a milestone in any woman's life?"

"I'd have a problem with the sun coming up in the west or waterfront property in Arizona, too. We're not discussing just 'any woman' here, we're discussing you and this afternoon, and what happened was more than just a little random groping."

"For you, maybe."

He shook his head and emitted a hoarse croak of a laugh. "You're good, lady. You're really good. You're going to play it cool, aren't you? Just pretend that this...whatever it is...between us doesn't exist."

"What it is," Susan said, "is just a little chemistry."

"A *little* chem—"

"And we just have to ignore—"

"We can't just ignore it, Steffie."

"We have to."

"We tried. It didn't work!"

The ramifications of his statement hung in the air between them like a cloud of stinging vapor. He had summed it up well: they had tried to ignore the attraction between them, and it hadn't worked. The time for denial or pretense was past; the fact of the attraction between them could no longer be suppressed. It must be faced.

Jumping frijoles! Susan thought frantically, how would Steffie have handled this?

By bringing in Victor Logan, of course, she decided. "Something's going to have to work," she said. "I'm...involved, and I have no intention of getting mixed up in some tacky triangle situation."

"Some tacky triangle?" he parroted incredulously. "What have you got now? Or haven't you given any thought to *Mrs*. Victor Logan? She's probably at the hospital plumping Logan's pillows, or sitting quietly at his bedside writing notes to acknowledge all his cards and flowers. You're already in a tacky triangle, Steffie. It's tacky because your side of the triangle is so short compared to Victor's and his wife's."

Susan didn't have to consciously consider what Steffie's reaction to this little speech might be.

"You're out of line, Haggerty. My personal life is no business of yours."

"Do you think I want it to be? If it weren't for...if I didn't find you attractive, your cockamamy personal life would be the last thing in the world I'd want to stick my nose in." He exhaled in exasperation. "As it is, you can't blame me for wondering why a woman like you would settle for being an unofficial second in any man's life."

"I'm not second in Victor's life."

"Then why aren't you at the hospital plumping his pillows and writing thank-you notes?"

Susan stiffened her spine. He'd gone too far. She was Steffie Meeks, and she was in charge. "You're quite impertinent, Haggerty. Before you say anything else, you might want to stop to consider that Victor Logan is your employer, and I am your acting supervisor. I would advise you to use a bit of discretion."

His eyes bored into her as he digested what she'd said. Susan swallowed the lump in her throat and resisted the urge to squirm under his piercing glare. The thought process was almost visible on his face as he evaluated their positions in this match. "You're bluffing, lady," he said finally. "You're not going to fire me. You'd have to explain it to Logan, and you can't afford to do that. You weren't the only one who got kissed today."

Susan's cheeks were burning. Haggerty was quick as a rattlesnake; he struck with lightning swiftness and chilling accuracy. He must never, *never* suspect that she was involved in a charade. He was a thorn in her side with the potential of becoming a lance. She bobbed her head deferentially, then forced herself to look straight into his eyes. "Touché, Haggerty. I think we can agree that forgetting about what happened this afternoon would be mutually beneficial."

"It wasn't a forgettable kiss," he said. His eyes locked with hers, and there was a communication between them that was explicit without requiring words. Susan's lips tingled with the memory of his lips on them, and she felt a warmth swirling deep inside her as her entire body recalled the feel of being held against a broad chest, of being caressed by strong arms.

Susan quietly swallowed the lump in her throat. "It mustn't happen again. We both have too much to lose. If you value your job, you'll do your level best to make sure it doesn't."

Her voice, croaky at first, gained strength as she spoke, until the admonition that he must prevent a recurrence of the storeroom incident took on the authoritative tone of an executive order and stung Clark's ego. He didn't like her down-the-nose attitude. He didn't like the fact that he was subject to her authority. Most of all, he didn't like the power she had to keep him in a perpetual state of arousal. Even now he was imagining what it would be like to kiss her again, was aching with the need to hold her. She was an enigma—a combination of soft, slippery satin and cold, hard steel. She mesmerized and enticed him, infuriated and frustrated him.

What was it about this woman that gave her the power to crawl inside his skin and play with his senses? She was a pretty woman, certainly, but the world was filled with beautiful women, and not one of them had ever strapped him into the seat of a roller coaster like the one he'd been riding since Steffie Meeks had shown up at the warehouse.

How deceptively innocent she looked in that flowery dress, with her damp hair drying into fluffy curls! God, how he'd love to pull her onto his lap and wrap his arms around her and whisper some silly something in her ear that would make her laugh. He would nibble at her rather delectable neck and ferret out her earlobe and get lost in the scent of whatever it was she wore that smelled so clean and fresh.

Her voice, which he knew could be melodious, was sharp as she interrupted his fantasy. "Do we have an understanding?" she asked.

"An understanding?"

For a bright man he was certainly being obtuse, Susan thought. "I asked if we had an understanding. If you value your job, you'll see to it that what happened this afternoon doesn't happen again."

"If it does," he said testily, impaling her with a piercing glare, "it won't be at my initiation."

Susan's jaw dropped open, and she snapped it shut. Of all the smug, pompous . . . devilishly handsome men! He had to be taken down a notch. It was her *duty* to knock some of that cocksureness out of

him. "Then there's absolutely no danger of anything happening," she said, rising from the chair,
"and there's nothing more to talk about. You came
to clear the air, Haggerty, and now it's clear."

"Crystal clear," he growled, smarting from the
abrupt dismissal. He followed her to the door, wishing he could resist watching the sway of her hips beneath the flowing fabric of her dress as she walked.

"Have a nice weekend," she said, opening the
door for him and standing next to it with her arms
akimbo like a night club bouncer who'd invited a
rowdy drunk to leave.

"Thank you, Ms. Meeks," he said, sarcastic respect heavy in his voice. "I plan to."

Lordy, Susan thought, wincing as the door
slammed shut behind him, Haggerty did get testy
when subjected to authority!

The phone rang before she had even finished un-
lacing Steffie's sandals.

"You must be a lousy hostess," Peter opened
without preamble. "I just saw your guest leave, and
he didn't look happy."

Susan laughed. "He wasn't."

"How did it go?"

"I handled it."

"You sound proud of yourself."

"Even you would have been proud of me," she
said. "I'm not Clark Haggerty's favorite person right
now, but there's no doubt in his mind whom he's
dealing with or who's in charge."

Chapter Five

Clark would have enjoyed the feel of a cool breeze on his face as he stalked away from Steffie's condo, but the weather was unseasonably warm and perversely humid, even for Houston. There were names for women like Steffie Meeks, names and adjectives—wonderful, delectable, cathartic adjectives that paraded through his mind in a seemingly endless file as he walked.

Kiss her again? That dominating female, that . . . He reached the amenities area and directed a scowl at the redwood tub filled with hot, bubbling water. Her specter stood on the deck, dressed in a shimmering green swimsuit, blotting wet skin with a towel. Damn her. Hell, yes, he'd kiss her. And more.

If she weren't dead set on throwing her life away on Victor Logan.

The thing that really nettled him was the incredible stupidity of it. It didn't fit. A woman like Steffie—young, beautiful, smart, *gentle*—wasting herself on a man twice her age and married. A selfish old coot who'd buy her expensive trinkets and, if she were lucky, set up some confidential trust fund for her in the event of his death, but who'd leave her a spinster just past her prime, slinking unobtrusively into the back pew of the church during his funeral service.

Why? Why did she settle for being his mistress? Was it the red Corvette and the condo with a hot tub? In spite of her reserve and her occasional shrewishness, Steffie didn't strike him as the type of woman who would sell herself for a car and a tub of water. There had to be another reason.

A frown dragged at the features of his face. The answer was obvious. And repugnant. She was really hung up on Logan. And, loving him, she was too blind to see how her relationship with him limited her, too loyal to him to admit what a selfish jerk he was for keeping her in an exploitive situation. If he cared for her, truly cared for her, he'd either sacrifice what had to be sacrificed to marry her, or he'd let her go.

Poor kid. Too naive to realize she was being used and abused and headed for a disastrous fall. She'd been young, inexperienced and ambitious when she'd met Logan, vulnerable to seduction on several levels. The attention of a successful man like Logan must have flattered her, and the opportunity for a shortcut up the corporate ladder would have been a powerful lure. Then, once she had taken the bait, she was hooked. After the luster of an executive assistantship and a company Corvette had worn off, she was too involved to extricate herself from Logan and Logan International.

Poor kid, he thought again, remembering the timidity that often lurked in the green depths of her eyes. She was running in place, and she'd have to take a giant step backward to get off the treadmill—one very scary giant step down and back to square one.

The whole ridiculous situation suddenly seemed unbearable to him. Here he was, fuming over a woman who didn't have enough sense to pull herself out of a bad situation, a woman headed for disaster. He was not, by nature, a fumer; he was a doer. And there was nothing he could do about Steffie Meeks's bleak future. Steffie was the only person who could help Steffie, and she was too blind to lead herself out of the fog.

Or was she? He pondered the question as he drove. Perhaps she was only wearing blinders. Maybe deep down she knew she was in trouble and didn't know how to get out. The way she'd kissed him—before she'd messed it up with the crack about Logan and he'd messed it up even further—that first kiss had been genuine. The chemistry between them was incredibly strong, but if she really loved Logan, and if that love was fulfilling to her, she wouldn't have been so susceptible to chemistry with another man. She was reaching for something, searching for it, yet every time she reached for it the effort scared her, and she retreated into that arrogant aloofness.

Damn it. She'd just chopped his ego in half, deliberately, and still he ached for her. His physical response to her had always been immediate and intense, but since he'd kissed her, he felt something more than physical, something that made him want to know Steffie Meeks, not as a boss or another man's mistress or as a short-term lover, but as a woman, a confidante and friend. He wanted to get inside Steffie's head, her heart and her soul.

A self-deprecatory smile curved his lips. He wouldn't complain about getting into her bed along the way.

The smile faded quickly, to be replaced by a brooding scowl. He wasn't going to get anywhere with her until she saw this thing with Logan for what it was, and he didn't have time to wait around for her great awakening. She was the type of woman who could stick with Logan for years out of some oddball sense of loyalty.

No, he thought, he couldn't wait around for any gradual awakening. But the process might be speeded up with the right person pointing out a few obvious truths to her—to nurture the seedlings of doubt already planted in her mind.

He considered the prospect a moment. Yes, he should be able at least to *start* her thinking about what her relationship with Logan was costing her, and where she was headed if she remained in it. He rather fancied the idea of rescuing Steffie Meeks from herself. It seemed like a heroic quest. Of course, he'd have to proceed cautiously, being careful about when he pushed and when he slackened the pressure. He couldn't afford to alienate her too much, or he'd end up blowing both his job and any chance to get closer to her in one fell swoop. But if he was careful enough...

Susan clawed at the shrink wrap that sealed a twelve-bottle pack of correction fluid and mused, Why is it every time I need something from this storeroom it's either on the top shelf or packaged securely enough to withstand a nuclear blast? Persistence paid off finally, and she took a bottle from the pack and slid the carton back onto the shelf.

Without warning, a menacing, inhuman hiss sounded from the dark, hidden spaces at the back of the shelf, and an enormous beast with long black fur flew past her head, brushing her shoulder with its feet and her face with its fur as it skittered to the floor and disappeared in a dark blur. Susan didn't think; she had a reaction similar to the startled animal's—she screamed.

Clark's concentration on his work had been suffering since he'd seen Steffie leave her office and heard the squeak of the storeroom door being opened. The thought of Steffie in that room had stirred distracting memories. At the sound of her scream, so unexpected and urgent, he bolted out of his chair and dashed toward the storeroom, then heaved a sigh of relief when a streak of black fur catapulted past his feet en route to the stairs.

Still shaken, Susan was leaning against a shelf for support, trying to breathe in enough air to force her heart out of her throat and back to her chest where it belonged. She limply acknowledged Clark's presence as he appeared in the doorway. He shrugged. "I heard you scream. Are you . . . ?"

She turned wild, wide green eyes toward him. "There was a huge rat," she said, still breathless. "It—" screwing up her face in disgust, she finished "—*touched* me." She squared her shoulders and made an executive decision. "I'm calling an exterminator. Immediately."

Clark threw back his head and produced a deep rumble of masculine laughter. "That wasn't a rat, Steffie. It was Jezebel, our watch cat."

"A cat?" Susan said, then repeated, incredulously, "A *cat*?"

"She's half wild, but she keeps the rodent population under control. She steers clear of us humans whenever possible, but every once in a while she comes leaping out at someone."

"That . . . creature . . . has a name?"

"Umm," Clark said. "Jezebel. I'm surprised you haven't heard about her. According to the guys on the dock, she's an institution here."

"I don't shoot the breeze with the guys on the dock too often," she said wryly.

He cocked a censorious eyebrow at her. "No. I don't suppose you do."

Smarting from the condemnation in his tone of voice, she asked irritably, "Is that little beast vaccinated and spayed?"

"She's not a pet, Steffie. She just lives here and keeps the mice away."

"If she bites someone, they'd have to go through the entire rabies series. LIFT could be liable."

"True," Clark said, "but catching her would be next to impossible."

"How does your schedule look? Can we take care of it today?"

"You're really serious about this, aren't you? You want to chase down that half-wild cat and drag it off to the vet."

Susan had to fight to keep a straight face. My, but bowing to authority went against Clark Haggerty's grain. The hint of a dimple appeared in his cheek as he set his mouth in a petulant line. "Someone should have done it long ago," she said.

"Victor's never been concerned over Jezebel," he rebutted grumpily. On a scale of one to ten, chasing down Jezebel rated about a minus twenty in his priorities. Trust a woman to come up with a harebrained idea. And this woman would follow through with it.

"Victor gets too busy looking at the big picture to notice the brushstrokes," she said, flashing him a devastatingly sweet smile. "Besides, Victor is indisposed, and I'm in charge. Is there anything pressing you have to take care of this morning?

"No," he admitted grudgingly.

"Then I suggest you get a flashlight and find Jezebel while I look up a vet in the yellow pages."

Jaw clenched, he watched her walk away. She was wearing a gabardine skirt that fit snugly across her derriere. Nice. If she weren't so disgustingly cute when she lorded her authority over him, if there weren't a glint of mischief in the emerald sparkle of her eyes when she flexed her corporate muscles, he would cheerfully have strangled her. But she *was* cute, and he did sense a trace of humor in her dictatorship, and as much as he hated the thought of taking orders from her, he found himself wanting her more after each of their confrontations. No wonder Victor Logan didn't want to let her go.

Damn Logan! he thought as he started down the concrete steps. The man should be drawn and quartered for what he was doing to her life.

Steffie hung up the phone and went in search of Clark. He was just stepping up on the bottom step of the stairs as she reached the top. "I found a vet who can take us right away. Did you find Jezebel?"

"The dock crew pointed me in the right direction. I found her, all right. Getting her out is going to be another matter. We'd better get a box ready for her or we'll have a tiger by the tail with no place to put it."

They punched air holes in the side of a corrugated shipping carton, and Clark carried it to the base of a wire-rung ladder that led to a loft storage area. "You're going to have to follow me up to hold the light. Can you manage?"

She nodded. "I'll just have to take off my shoes."

"Let's get going."

"Wait." She stopped him by putting her hand on his forearm. Her skin was soft and smooth and cooler than his, and he was suddenly aware of the scent of her perfume. "You can't go after her in a short-sleeved shirt. Don't you have a jacket or parka or something you could wear to protect your arms?"

He shrugged. "I think there're a couple hanging near the check station. I suppose a little precaution would make sense."

"You'll need some safety glasses from over in the crating room."

His smile was beautiful. There was no other way to describe it. It softened rough, handsome features into pure, artistic, masculine perfection that sent her senses spinning. He said, "Anyone ever tell you you'd make a great mother?"

She grinned self-consciously and said offhandedly, "I wouldn't want you getting hurt and suing LIFT."

Brown eyes caressed her face, and he ran his index finger over her forearm from elbow to wrist, then leaned over to whisper in her ear, "I don't think it's LIFT you're worried about."

She lowered her head and forced herself to shrug. "I don't like to see anyone hurt unnecessarily."

Clark cradled her chin with his fingertips and guided her face up so that their eyes met. The time had come to water some of the seedling doubts. "You'll never have children with Logan," he said. "Babies wouldn't fit into his life." Before she could answer, he dropped his hand, turned and walked off to get the jacket and glasses.

Susan exhaled heavily, feeling herself shrivel inside like a deflating balloon. So Haggerty had decided Logan was bad for her. Damn it! For a minor complication, Haggerty was turning into a major problem. The crack about Logan had caught her unprepared. If he continued in that vein, she was going to have to go for his jugular, and she didn't like manufacturing ill will between them. In addition to being attracted to Haggerty, she was beginning to like him. Sexual chemistry was dangerous enough in a vacuum; it was a tempest when paired with growing affection.

She had the racing pulse to prove it.

He was back soon, wearing a blue jacket with the LIFT logo on it and holding safety glasses, a flashlight and a quilted shipping blanket.

"Expecting a cold front?" she asked.

"It's for the cat. If I can get her wrapped in it, she should calm down enough for us to get her in the box."

Susan giggled. "You'd think we were on a big-game hunt."

Haggerty's grim grin was ingratiating. "It's your safari, lady, not mine."

Halfway up the wire ladder, he turned and complained, "This wasn't on the job description when I took the job."

"Just catch the cat, Haggerty."

He reached the loft, slid the box to one side and settled back on his haunches under the low ceiling. Susan stopped on the second rung from the top, her head and shoulders just above the floor of the narrow space, and looked around the dusty area, wrinkling her nose in disgust. "When was the last time anyone cleaned up here?"

"There's probably sawdust here from the original construction. This area isn't used much."

"It's hot up here."

"Uh-huh. And *you're* not wearing a jacket. Let's get the light on so she can get used to it."

"What's this?" Susan asked, pointing at a plastic fast-food carton filled with brown chunks of something.

"Cat food. The men put some up here every few days for the kitten."

"Kitten?"

"Uh-huh. Seems Jezebel doesn't live the lonely life she'd have us believe. She had three this litter, but the loading dock workers have found homes for two of them, so there's only one left."

"I want to see it."

"You'll probably get a glance at it." He clicked on the flashlight and scanned the beam slowly across the floor of the loft, stopping it finally when it landed on Jezebel. She was sitting on a pile of burlap, with the proud countenance of a queen holding court.

"She didn't bolt. That's a promising sign," he whispered. "Now, if you'll hold the light so I can ease up to her..."

Despite his size, he moved gracefully and noiselessly in the low space. Jezebel sat perfectly still in the flashlight's glare, defiantly defending her burlap throne. On close inspection, she was quite a handsome cat, with a silky long-haired coat, black expect for a spot of vivid white on her chest. In a flicker of movement, a miniature Jezebel poked its head up from the folds of the rough cloth, blinked at the beam of light and mewed, winning itself a new home and mistress.

Clark, oblivious to the kitten's antics, froze about a yard away from Jezebel and began pleating the quilt into his hands, positioning it to be flung over the momma cat. He sprang so fast that Jezebel didn't have a chance of escape, and even Susan, who was expecting the action, was startled. His crawl back to the ladder was considerably faster than his approach to the cat had been.

Entwined in the folds of the blanket, Jezebel fought with the spirit of a Tasmanian devil, and her hissing and spitting were audible even through the quilting. "Get the box open," Clark said urgently.

He shoved both blanket and cat inside, and Susan held the flaps down against the cat's efforts at escape. "Mission accomplished," Clark said. "I'm just glad I'm not the one who has to give her a shot."

"As long as you're up here, you might as well get the kitten."

Clark blotted the thin layer of perspiration on his forehead with the back of his hand. "You've got to be kidding."

"I'm not kidding. I want it. The kids—" In her effort to swallow the slip of tongue, she almost broke skin biting the inside of her lip. "I know some kids who would want it," she said quickly. "They had to have their cat put to sleep a few months ago."

He was sitting on the floor with one leg extended, the other bent, his arm draped over the bent knee. "Shouldn't you call their mother before you go taking a kitten to their house? She may not want—"

"I know their mother. She's been trying to find a kitten for them."

"Very well," he said, frowning as he shifted back into a crawling position.

"You certainly grumble a lot, Haggerty," she said with a tinkle of laughter.

"Only in the face of insanity," he retorted.

She wondered, as she watched him crawl away, how she'd never noticed what powerful legs he had— firm and muscular under the taut fabric of his pants. He lunged for the kitten, caught it, and immediately a scathing expletive filled the air.

"Problems?" she said airily.

"This little hellcat is her mother's offspring. She got me good."

"How do you know it's a she?"

"Her temperament," he said dryly.

The subject of their discussion meowed, and Jezebel launched a fresh assault at the walls of the box. Susan and Clark both leaped to secure the lid. Clark's brisk movement inadvertently surprised the kitten, who mewed again and raked its small but lethal claws over the top of his hand. Clark called it a choice name.

"For Pete's sake, give me that kitten before you scare her to death," Susan said, and cradled the ball of fluff to her breast, anchoring it there with one hand. She petted it with the fingertips of her other hand, cooing reassurances to it.

The seductive tone of her voice made Clark forget his battle wounds. He shook his head in exasperation. "Let's get downstairs. It's hot up here. Can you manage with the kitten?"

Susan was already two steps down. "Cuddles and I will be fine. Just make sure you keep the lid on that box closed. There's some packing tape in my office. We'll secure it with that."

His only reply was a disgruntled harrumph.

Still nestling the kitten against her bosom, she held the box lid closed with her free hand while Clark taped it shut. Drops of blood were beading over the criss-cross of scratches on the top of his hand.

Susan touched the side of his hand with her forefinger. He froze, his eyes meeting hers significantly. Susan swallowed the lump that had formed suddenly in her throat and said, "We've got to get these cuts cleaned. I saw a first-aid kit in the storeroom."

"It's just a few scratches."

"Go wash your hands with warm soapy water, and I'll get the first-aid kit."

"I don't suppose it would do any good to argue with Mother Meeks."

"None at all."

While he was away she found a box for the kitten and was waiting for Clark with a bottle of iodine and a gauze pad when he returned from the washroom. "Did you use soap?" she asked with exaggerated condescension.

He answered with a scowl.

"Good boy," she said. "Now give me your hand so I can paint it."

"Iodine?"

"Uh-huh."

Grudgingly he extended his hand. "What's wrong with peroxide?"

"It wouldn't sting enough. Besides, there wasn't any in the first-aid kit." He winced as she pressed the gauze to the cuts and, spontaneously, she blew on them the way she did with her children's injuries.

The sight of her pursed lips, the feel of her breath gliding over his hand, elicited a response in him far removed from the stinging wounds. Susan sensed his attention on her and raised her eyes to encounter brown ones filled with a raw, sexual yearning. An answering wave of excitement shuddered through her.

Following a moment of stultified paralysis, she forced her eyes from his and turned away from him. Finally, with the sluggish motion of a B-movie zombie, she tossed the used gauze pad into the wastebasket, then dropped her arms limply to her sides. She didn't move as he stepped behind her and said in a near whisper, "You're too much a woman to live with a man's leftovers."

Words she wanted to say came out as a hoarse croak. She closed her mouth, swallowed, tried again. "Please don't say things like that."

His hand lighted on her shoulder with the grace of a leaf fluttering on a breeze and rested there, solid and strong. She inhaled sharply. God, but he had a way of touching her that made her want to be touched more.

"You don't want to hear things like that because you're afraid of the truth," he said. "You're holding on to a dream that isn't real out of some misguided sense of loyalty. Let go of it, Steffie. Victor Logan isn't a dream. He's an anchor weighing you down."

"It's none of your business, Haggerty."

No, he thought. But he'd like to make it his business. He'd like to put his arms around her and kiss her until everything about her was his business, until Victor Logan wasn't even an issue.

Awkward silence stretched seconds into what seemed like hours before, ever so slowly, the charge of the atmosphere dissipated. Clark's voice was heavy as he spoke. "You don't need my help getting Jezebel to the vet. I'm going back to work."

Susan didn't move until he came into view through the glass wall between their offices and sat down at his desk, judiciously ignoring her.

Chapter Six

Absolutely not," Peter said. "We absolutely cannot bring Clark Haggerty into this job. He's an unknown factor."

"He's not an unknown factor," Susan countered, staring at him from across the condo's living room. "He's very efficient and—"

"The fewer people involved in any operation, the better, Susan. There's no justification for letting Haggerty in on this. Civilians aren't cut out for this type of work. They get caught up in the drama of it all and they tend to be indiscreet."

"Indiscreet? A man like Haggerty would let someone cut off his fingers knuckle by knuckle before he'd break a confidence."

"You can tell that just by working with him?"

"I can tell it just by talking to him."

"Damn it, Susan, you're a big girl. You knew the ground rules when you accepted this assignment. Now because things are getting a little chummy between you and Haggerty, you want to go letting the cat out of the bag."

Susan laughed a little hysterically, and Peter exhaled an exasperated sigh. "I'm glad you find some amusement in this debacle. Mind sharing the joke? I could use a good laugh."

"It was just the phrase you used," she said. "'Letting the cat out of the bag.' You should have seen him crawling up in that loft, shaking his head like he thought I'd gone mad."

"An astute observation," Peter said dryly. "Don't you think you carried that a bit far?"

"You told me to assert my authority, and I asserted it. He doesn't give me many opportunities. He's usually on top of his job without any nagging from me."

"Next you'll be telling me he wears a shirt with an *S* on the front and flies around in a cape."

"He's a good man, Peter. With integrity. We could trust him on this." Peter's stare was unyielding as she offered her last argument: "I don't like lying to him. He's too decent."

The stare became an interrogatory glare. "How serious is it?"

Her eyes narrowed. "What do you mean?"

"Are you in love with him?"

"Don't be ridiculous. He's just...I..."

Peter walked to the bar. "I'm going to get both of us a drink, Susie Cuke. You look as though you could use one, and I know I could."

"What did you call me?"

"Don't tell me you haven't heard it. All the men at the bridge call you Susie Cuke. Cuke, short for 'cucumber,' as in 'cool as.'"

She leaned her head against the back of the sofa and sighed. "I hadn't heard it. So they think I'm—"

"It's nothing personal," he said. "Just sour grapes. Every one of them would give a month's wages to get to first base with you, and not one of them has been able to." He brought her a stemmed snifter. "This ought to clean the cobwebs out of your chimney."

She took a sip and choked. "What is this?"

"A very expensive brandy," he said. "Steffie certainly knows how to stock a bar."

Setting the glass on the coffee table, she said, "It's too strong."

"Drink it, Susan. Orders. I have a feeling you're more shaken by what you've just learned about yourself than I am. And I, young lady, am considerably shaken. This was the last snafu I expected on this job."

"No. I don't suppose you could be expected to anticipate that Susie Cool-as-a-Cucumber might actually get interested in a man. You must have found it difficult keeping a straight face when I told you that he'd kissed me."

Peter grinned that boyish, teddy-bear grin. "Jeez, Susan, I figured you'd heard the name. It's so ridiculous it doesn't bear repeating except in an ironic way. And you're not the first agent to fall in love in the middle of an undercover operation."

"I'm not in love with him. I just…respect him as a fellow human being."

"Whatever it is you feel about him is totally unimportant to this job. What matters is keeping the percolator plugged in so the coffee can perk. After we nab our man down south, you can work things out with Haggerty any way you like. Until then, you're to maintain the status quo."

Susan sighed wearily. "What am I doing here playing secret agent, Peter? I should be home with my kids. Greg is down with a cold, Kara's been selected for a part in a PTO program and I'm going to miss it. And Mom sounds exhausted from running after them."

"Drink your brandy, Susan, then go have a long soak in the hot tub, or a good cry, and get a good night's sleep. You'll be home in a couple of weeks, and everything will pick up where you left off."

She chose to have the good cry while soaking in the privacy of her whirlpool. She cried because she missed her kids and the comfortable routine of home, because she didn't want to go back to the warehouse and pretend to be Steffie Meeks anymore and because she was all mixed up where Haggerty was concerned.

It was unfair, the power men had to complicate a woman's life! She'd been very happy dividing her energy between her job and her family until Tyler had decided to switch from friendship to courtship, recruiting her own mother as chief advocate in his campaign to get her to marry him. She'd taken this job to escape the pressure for a while, and as soon as she'd made a definitive decision about what to do about Tyler, she'd met Clark Haggerty. Damn!

She hadn't been able to imagine Tyler in this sunken bathtub with her, to conjure up some excitement at the thought of such intimacy with him. And because she couldn't, she saw that as evidence that she had no business thinking about marrying him.

Excitement didn't begin to describe what she felt when she found herself imagining—against her will—being in this setting with Clark Haggerty. It was more than excitement; it was a tingling awareness, a sense-reeling anticipation, an urgent need to see the fantasy become reality.

But if feeling no buzz of excitement over the idea of a sexual liaison with Tyler was enough to convince her that she shouldn't marry him, then what the hell were all these fantasies about Haggerty supposed to mean?

Susan didn't want to think about it. Thrusting cupped hands into the tub, she filled them with water and doused her face, washing away tears of frustration. She simply *refused* to think about it now.

Mere seconds later she climbed out of the oval tub and wondered what it would feel like to have Clark

Haggerty kiss the back of her neck while he wrapped Steffie's velour bath blanket around her shoulders.

Clark dropped tiredly onto the worn sofa, a dog-eared book in one hand, a white, grease-stained paper bag in the other. There was a table in the breakfast nook, a discard from one of his sister's neighbors who'd been redecorating about the time Clark had set up his apartment, but he didn't feel like staring at the empty chair across from his when he was eating take-out fast food. It seemed, somehow, almost like hypocrisy. In any event, the light was better for reading on the sofa.

Styrofoam French fries and a cardboard hamburger added up to an unappetizing meal, and the intricacies of international tariff regulations were poor dinner companions, so the meal did little to lift his sagging spirits. He slapped the book shut scarcely half an hour after finishing what could loosely be termed his food. He should have read at least another chapter, but he was unable to concentrate and knew that reading would be a wasted effort in the frame of mind he was in.

A layer of dust on the particle-board shelving holding his stereo caught his eye. Eventually he was going to have to devote half a Saturday to cleaning the place up. Not that it would do any good, really. He could move the dust and ruffle the dilapidated carpets with the vacuum cleaner, but it would still be a depressing box with plaster walls—hardly what one would call home. God, he was looking forward to leaving this place for something bigger and better, investing in some furniture, collecting some luxurious extras. A fireplace would be nice for atmosphere, perhaps a leather recliner for comfort and a wet bar for entertaining.

A fluffy rug in front of the fireplace, stemmed glasses filled with wine reflecting the twinkling light of the fire, Steffie stretched out on the rug, training liquid green eyes on his face as he shared his most personal dreams...

With a growl of frustration, he dragged himself off the sofa and gathered up the carnage of paper bags, plastic containers and minute envelopes of salt and pepper left over from his meal. It wasn't late, certainly not too late to go out and find a place crowded with other human beings in need of companionship, some cozy little pub with backgammon boards and electronic games and music loud enough to muffle the chatter and laughter of people trying to relate with other human beings in some significant way.

But that prospect held little allure for him. Clark wasn't in the mood for the getting-to-know-you games and guarded small talk that went with those scenes. He had a hollow in his life that couldn't be filled up by strangers. Funny, he hadn't noticed how deep and wide that hollow had become until Steffie Meeks had come prancing into the LIFT warehouse. Since meeting her and getting lost in the enigma of her—the contrasts between shyness and brusqueness, authority and vulnerability—he'd begun to feel the walls of that vast emptiness in his life shifting,

sliding, eroding away, leaving the hollow larger and
larger.

The chasm of loneliness, so newly discovered, unsettled him. To fill it he needed Steffie, and the
prospect of letting someone invade the private re-
cesses of his life was frightening, even more so when
that someone was an unknown factor like Steffie
Meeks. The precarious balance of their present situation appeared as stable as a concrete slab when
compared to the prospects for a future with her.

The knowledge that he was out of control where
Steffie was concerned nettled him. It was Steffie who
must make the decisions and take the stands that
could open up the future for them. He was powerless to do anything but try to influence her decisions
and wait for her to act or not act.

And what if she made all the right choices? he
wondered. Whatever developed between them would
not be casual. Nothing between them ever had been.
Clark wasn't at all convinced he was ready for the
upheaval Steffie could affect in his life—he only
knew that if Steffie made the *wrong* choices, he
would forever regret not finding out what might have
happened between them.

God, how he despised the waiting, the pretense
that nothing was going on between them, when the
earth reeled under his feet every time he saw her. The
unguarded moments between them were so rich and
fine—he could so easily conjure up the image of her
smile, could feel the tenderness of her nature as she
cradled the kitten to her breast, could hear the mel-

ody of amusement in her voice as she bullied him
into going after Jezebel.

A tightness filled his chest at the thought of what
it would be like tomorrow at the warehouse. He and
Steffie would totter as if on a tightrope, tense and
miserable, to keep from shattering the fragile illusion that nothing significant was happening between them. Victor Logan—poor, sick Victor lan-
guishing in a hospital bed—would be a specter separating them, and the situation would remain un-
changed until Steffie was able to exorcise Logan
from her life and extricate herself from Logan International.

Clark sighed raggedly. *If* Steffie could find the
courage.

He went to bed aching with his need to have her
with him. She had to ditch Logan before it was too
late, he thought gravely. The alternative was unthinkable.

After the bustle of activity on the loading dock,
Clark was looking forward to the relative serenity of
his office. His clipboard was fat with the paperwork
involved in off-loading the parade of trucks that had
arrived that morning. Incoming shipments always
arrived in a feast-or-famine fashion, several at once
then none for half a day or more.

The door to Steffie's office was open, and he could
see that she was standing at the window overlooking
the dock. He knocked lightly on the doorjamb, and
she turned.

"Hope I'm not intruding," he said.

"Certainly not," she said. "What's up?"

"Nothing really. I just noticed you watching the dock and wondered if there was a problem."

"No," she said, turning back to the window. "It's just interesting when its busy, watching everyone at work, so many people doing so many things at once."

"We've got a pretty good crew. If we didn't, mornings like this one would be mayhem."

"Who's the woman?" she asked.

"Woman?" He stepped to the window and stood next to her, following her line of vision. "Oh, that's Lewis's wife. She brought his lunch."

Even from the distance it was easy to see that Mrs. Lewis was young, perhaps still in her teens, and had long, flowing hair, worn loose. She was in the later stages of pregnancy. The sight of her with her husband, sitting on a metal shipping crate with their brown paper lunch bag between them, brought back memories of similar indoor picnics with Greg in the back room of the car-rental office.

Watching her instead of the Lewises, Clark thought he'd never seen her look lovelier. He wondered what she was thinking about that softened the features of her face so.

"Does she bring his lunch often?" she asked.

"Once a week or so."

"How quaint," she said. The harshness of her voice was jarring, given the expression on her face. God, this woman was a riddle. She continued, her attitude getting sharper as she spoke. "It's against regulations having nonemployees on the dock, but I suppose it's not doing any harm as long as she leaves when the lunch hour's over."

He found the sudden callousness in her attitude offensive. "You're all heart, Miss Meeks."

Ouch! thought Susan, glad that the quick reversion to Steffie's perspective had worked. For a while she'd forgotten who she was supposed to be. "It could get to be a security problem if we had wives running in and out at will," she said. "Not to mention a safety problem. We wouldn't want a pregnant woman tripping over a cord or colliding with a forklift."

Clark's silence conceded the point she'd made, and for a while neither of them spoke. Clark knew he should leave, but he didn't want to. It was so much nicer being here next to her than playing peekaboo through the glass wall between their offices. Opportunities to talk to her were rare—by her design. He wanted to exploit this one. "What became of Jezebel's kitten?" he asked.

"She's taken over the guest room at my condo until her new owners get back from vacation. How's your hand?"

He held it up for her to see. "Healing nicely."

"Looks to me like it could use a fresh coat of iodine."

"You'd have to toss a blanket over me and throw me in a box first."

FIRST CLASS ROMANCE

Mail This Heart TODAY!

And We'll Deliver:

**4 FREE BOOKS
A FREE PEN & WATCH SET
PLUS
A SURPRISE MYSTERY BONUS
TO YOUR DOOR!**

See Inside For More Details →

SILHOUETTE DELIVERS FIRST-CLASS ROMANCE— DIRECT TO YOUR DOOR

Mail the Heart sticker on the postpaid order card today and you'll receive:

— **4 new Silhouette Romance novels—FREE**
— **an elegant pen & watch set—FREE**
— **and a surprise mystery bonus—FREE**

But that's not all. You'll also get:

Free Home Delivery

When you subscribe to Silhouette Romance, the excitement, romance and faraway adventures of these novels can be yours for previewing in the convenience of your own home. Every month we'll deliver 6 new books right to your door. If you decide to keep them, they'll be yours for only $1.95 each. And there is no extra charge for shipping and handling!

Free Monthly Newsletter

It's the indispensable insider's look at our most popular writers and their upcoming novels. Now you can have a behind-the-scenes look at the fascinating world of Silhouette! It's an added bonus you'll look forward to every month!

Special Extras—FREE

Because our home subscribers are our most valued readers, we'll be sending you additional free gifts from time to time as a token of our appreciation.

OPEN YOUR MAILBOX TO A WORLD OF LOVE AND ROMANCE EACH MONTH. JUST COMPLETE, DETACH AND MAIL YOUR FREE OFFER CARD TODAY!

FREE—digital watch and matching pen

You'll love your new LCD quartz digital watch with its genuine leather strap. And the slim matching pen is perfect for writing that special person. Both are yours FREE as our gift of love.

Silhouette Romance®

FREE OFFER CARD

4 FREE BOOKS

FREE HOME DELIVERY

PLACE HEART STICKER HERE

FREE PEN AND WATCH SET

FREE FACT-FILLED NEWSLETTER

FREE MYSTERY BONUS

MORE SURPRISES THROUGHOUT THE YEAR—FREE

☑ **YES!** Please send me four Silhouette Romance novels, **free**, along with my free pen & watch set and my free mystery gift as explained on the opposite page.

CMR047

NAME _____

ADDRESS _____ APT. _____

CITY _____ STATE _____

ZIP CODE _____

Terms and prices subject to change.
Your enrollment is subject to acceptance
by Silhouette Books.

SILHOUETTE "NO-RISK" GUARANTEE
• There is no obligation to buy—the free books and gifts remain yours to keep.
• You receive books before they're available in stores.
• You may end your subscription anytime—just let us know.

PRINTED IN U.S.A.

Remember! To receive your free books, pen and watch set and mystery gift, return the postpaid card below. But don't delay!

DETACH AND MAIL CARD TODAY.

If offer card has been removed, write to: Silhouette Books, 120 Brighton Road, P.O. Box 5084, Clifton, NJ, 07015-9956

BUSINESS REPLY MAIL

FIRST CLASS PERMIT NO. 194 CLIFTON, N.J.

Postage will be paid by addressee

**Silhouette Books
120 Brighton Road
P.O. Box 5084
Clifton, NJ 07015-9956**

NO POSTAGE
NECESSARY
IF MAILED
IN THE
UNITED STATES

A smile like his could break hearts, Susan thought,
and then she suddenly became very somber, realizing that her own heart was in jeopardy. She was ever
aware of the sheer virility of Clark Haggerty, and
being attracted to him in such a fundamental way
made her vulnerable. His smile, his deep male voice,
his unadulteratedly masculine reflexes held an irre-
sistible appeal for her. His potential to fill needs
she'd long suppressed constantly reminded her of
them. Yes, she could get used to basking in the warm
charm of his easy smile.

And why shouldn't she, at least temporarily?
There was no chance of anything between them going
beyond a comfortable coziness, so why not enjoy his
company while she had the chance? She had hair the
color of Steffie Meeks's hair and was wearing Steffie Meeks's clothes. Why not adopt Steffie's attitude of taking what you could get when it was
available? Clark Haggerty made her feel feminine
and desirable, two ways a woman had a right to feel,
so why not spend some time with him while she had
the opportunity?

"Would you consider letting LIFT buy you lunch
in lieu of a purple heart for your on-the-job injuries?" she asked.

Some things are handed to you on a platter, Haggerty thought. "As long as you don't come after me
with iodine again," he said evenly.

They went to Shanghai Red's and waited for a table next to the window. Annointed by the brilliant
sunlight that poured through the glass, Clark was

magnificently male. His large expressive eyes seemed
to absorb the light and twinkle with it as he spoke
animatedly. Susan was filled with a peculiar contentment when he gazed across the table at her. And
with that contentment came a knowledge, perversely certain, that her protestations to Peter had
been ashes thrown into the wind. She *was* in love
with Clark Haggerty. It was impossible and damned
inconvenient and would probably result in her heart
being broken, but it was fact.

Even while shell-shocked by her realization, Susan understood instinctively that any lasting relationship with him was out of the question. Even if
Clark were smitten with her—and he certainly was
attracted to her—it wasn't Susan Carlson he was re-
acting to but Steffie Meeks. Clark was intrigued by
a glamorous, worldly woman. Part of his attraction
to her, however subconscious in origin, was bound
to be because she was the mistress of a powerful man
and therefore desirable to all men.

Clark's voice drew her back to the present. "Have
you decided?"

Decided? she thought. Decided what I'm going to
do about loving you? I'm simply going to savor every
moment with you until reality comes crashing down
between us. "I'll have the seafood salad," she said.

"Where were we?" Clark said as the waiter took
their menus.

"You were going to tell me what you do when
you're not managing the LIFT warehouse," she said.

"Not a whole lot," he said. "I'm taking some courses that keep me pretty busy. So between work and school and study, I really lead a rather dull life."

"What kind of courses?"

"One of them concerns export tariffs," he said vaguely. "I thought it would be good background information."

"Where do you go to school?"

"Downtown."

"I've heard UH's downtown campus has been expanding." Actually, she'd read it—in the Chamber of Commerce propaganda Peter had given her so she could familiarize herself with Houston.

"What about you?" he said. "What do you do after work?"

You mean besides laundry and supervising homework and chauffeuring the kids to assorted birthday parties or taking in an occasional movie? she thought wryly. She said, "When I'm not anticipating stolen moments with Victor, you mean?"

Her voice was strangely devoid of rancor when she said it, and Clark, not wanting to spoil the time with her, let it pass. At the moment he was too absorbed in her beauty for argument. Her flawless features, naturally pretty, withstood the test of bright sunlight, and the sunshine landed on her hair like a halo, sparking highlights in the apricot tint. But it was her eyes that drew him the most, purely green as the polished leaves of a pampered plant. He saw the real Steffie Meeks in those eyes, not the tough, callous person she sometimes pretended to be. There was an ocean in her eyes that he could drown in.

His refusal to lift up the gauntlet she'd tossed at him set the tone for the rest of the meal. They chatted about inconsequential matters, comfortable with each other, while a current of sexual awareness flowed to and fro between them, heightening their senses.

By the end of the meal they were sated in more ways than one. Certainly they were no longer hungry, but just as the food had fed their bodies, the easy camaraderie between them had nourished their emotional need for closeness. The sexual energy between them, still strong, was no longer an exclusively chemical reaction of male to female. Names, faces, *individuals* were involved. Clark longed to know Steffie intimately, Susan yearned to know Clark, and the knowledge they were seeking went beyond physical consummation.

They were especially aware of each other's presence in the compact sports car as Susan drove back to the warehouse. Their arms brushing as they sat in the small seats, the scents of perfume and after-shave mingling together, the soft music playing on the tape deck all created a rarefied, sensual atmosphere. They rode most of the way in comfortable silence, with Susan watching the traffic and Clark idly studying Steffie's hands on the steering wheel.

Just blocks from the warehouse, Susan said, "Victor will be glad to hear business is picking up. How many trucks did you off-load?"

"Seven," he said, stiffening at the mention of
Logan. "How is Logan, anyway? Is he recovering?"

Victor Logan, except for the frustration of con-
finement, was living a damned easy life sequestered
in the private hospital room watching movies on a
VCR and reading the *Wall Street Journal*. Lying to
Clark distressed Susan now more than ever before.
"He's getting out of the hospital and going home
soon," she told him.

Clark felt the distance Victor Logan had put between them. As close together as they were in the
small car, they were suddenly a vast distance apart.
Misery, plainly visible, hardened her features when
she spoke of him. He paused, not knowing whether
to say something benign like he was glad to hear Logan was improving, or whether to seize this opportunity to drive home a point—and at the same time
destroy what was left of the intimacy they'd been
sharing.

What the hell? he decided. The intimacy had been
shot the moment Victor Logan's name rolled off her
lips. "What's wrong, Steffie? You should be dancing over his improvement."

"I'm—" she said, but he wouldn't let her continue.

"You can't stand the idea of his going home to his
wife, can you? She's going to have him exclusively
until he's recovered, and she could hardly welcome
you visiting him there. So you're stuck out on the

fringes, while Victor's wife and family hold his hand."

Susan's hands were now gripping the steering wheel so tightly that her knuckles were white. "Please don't."

"Please don't what, Steffie? Don't put voice to the unpalatable truth you're wrestling with? Don't put into words all your frustrations over not having a legitimate place in Logan's life? We're not supposed to talk about it, are we? But the pain in your face says it as plainly as anything I could say."

Tears she couldn't shed burned Susan's eyes. Oh, God, how this deception was tearing her up inside! He was so sincere—and so duped. When he learned the truth about who she was, he was going to despise her for letting him make such a fool of himself, yet she was powerless to do anything except stare at the road ahead and let him go on: Don Quixote Haggerty tilting at a windmill named Logan.

They reached the warehouse, and when the car's engine was cut off a roaring silence descended over them. Susan grabbed her purse and walked briskly toward the warehouse door. It took Clark a few seconds to work his long legs from the cramped quarters of the small car, but before she opened the door he caught up with her and put his hand on her shoulder. She froze in midstep but didn't look at him.

"Logan's cheating you," he said. "A woman like you deserves better. You need a man who'll make a place for you in his life, a place reserved only for you."

Still unable to face him, she stared at the doorknob her hand was grasping and said, "You don't know what you're talking about, Haggerty. You don't know anything about it."

He drew his hand away from her shoulder and saw her shudder in relief—or resignation. "I would make a place for you," he said flatly.

The commitment in the statement stunned them both. Susan's throat was so tight she had to fight for breath. How sweet it would be to hear him say that knowing who she was instead of believing her to be someone else! Every instinct in her yearned to turn and throw her arms around him and cling to him and beg him to make that place for her. But she remained motionless, muscles tight and chest aching as she fought against yielding to that impulse.

After what seemed an eternity, he said, "Think about it, Steffie. Think about it while you're sleeping alone in that fancy condo of yours, remembering that Logan is at home snuggling up to his wife, and ask yourself if you wouldn't choose a warm, caring body next to yours over that prestigious address."

Another eternity passed before Susan could gather the strength to pull open the door and step through it. She let it close behind her, leaving Clark staring at it and wondering if he was tilting at windmills.

Chapter Seven

Late that afternoon, Clark brought the paperwork from the morning shipments to Susan's office and silently laid them on her desk. Susan stopped what she was doing, looked up and gravely nodded an acknowledgment. Clark returned the nod and turned, but he hesitated momentarily as though he might turn around and say something, then he walked out the door in brisk, deliberate strides.

Susan exhaled heavily, sharing the frustrated dejection she had seen in the droop of his shoulders. How were they ever going to endure another week or more under this pressure? It was so difficult to deal with the knowledge that he was close by, within sight if she raised her head and looked into his office.

Through the connecting wall Susan heard Clark's phone buzz and, after stealing a glance at him as he answered it, she forced her attention to the stack of papers he had left on her desk. Seconds later she heard his footsteps on the concrete landing and then on the stairs.

She resumed her paperwork, reading each of the inventories, the name of the company sending each shipment and the intended destination. About halfway through the stack she stopped, frozen. A prickling sensation crawled over her scalp as she read again the name she had been looking for since arriving at LIFT: the name of the kingpin in South America and the corporation that received all the doctored shipments packed with currency. Suddenly the job she was doing became more than an abstract concept. No longer a game she was going to play, it was going to happen, for real, just as the kingpin's name was printed on the form in black letters on white paper. And she had been entrusted with a pivotal role in this real-life drama.

Disciplining trembling fingers into action, she flipped through the card file on the desk until she found the phone number she needed, and dialed it. A very crisp, efficient voice answered, and she replied, "I'd like to leave a message for Mr. Cruz, please."

"Certainly," said the answering-service voice.

"Please tell him the order he has been waiting on has come in, and he should contact his freight agent immediately."

The voice read the message back. "Do you want to leave a phone number?"

"He has it." After hanging up the phone, she propped her elbows on the desk and buried her face in her hands. Her heart was racing. Today was Thursday. If everything went as projected, the shipment would be doctored the following Wednesday afternoon, when the LIFT warehouse was closed. Six days, and her role in this intrigue would be finished.

She sighed woefully into her hands, stroking her eyebrows with her fingertips. Six days, and she'd never see Haggerty again.

The truck was a small one and the delivery even smaller. Within minutes Clark was headed back to his office, clipboard in hand. But his mind was not on the crates that had just been unloaded. It was on Steffie Meeks, and on the anguish in her eyes when she'd looked up at him from Logan's desk, seeming so small behind that absurdly wide expanse of veneer, like a tiny bird perched precariously on the edge of a large snowdrift. He'd wanted so badly to walk around that barrier and hold her, but she hadn't given him the necessary encouragement. She wasn't ready yet to forgive the messenger for carrying bad news.

After reaching the landing, he served himself a cup of coffee and walked toward her office, intending to offer to fill one for her. He needed to talk to her, even if just briefly.

Some instinct stopped him from passing through the door. Steffie was sitting there, pitifully distraught, with her face buried in her hands, and just when he was debating whether to enter her office or pass by it, a woeful sigh escaped from behind the curtain of her hands.

He set the cup of coffee on her desk, inches from her face and, surprised, she lifted her head.

"You look as though you could use a cup."

She could have used a hug instead, but she thanked him lamely and picked up the cup and took a sip.

"It's not bad news, is it?" he asked. "From the hospital?"

"No," she said weakly.

"I'm glad it's not that," he said sincerely. If Logan had suddenly decided to kick the bucket, she'd never speak to him again after the things he'd said that afternoon. "Steffie," he said, wanting to comfort her, no matter was the problem was.

"I . . . uh . . . just have a headache."

"Can I . . . is there anything I can get you?"

She shook her head. The soft, resigned sigh she made as she leaned her forehead against her fingertips again tugged at his heart. He didn't want to leave her, but she obviously didn't want his help, so he said, "I'll be in my office if you need anything," and left.

His spirits sagged as he sank into his chair. Steffie must be considering what he had thrown at her about her relationship with Logan. The truth of the arguments he'd presented were beginning to sink in, and fighting with herself over her attachment to Logan and loyalty to her own interests was tearing her up inside.

Well, Haggerty, he chastised himself, *are you pleased with your handiwork? She's in there tied up in knots because of your crusade. Your good intentions have succeeded in making the lady miserable.*

After mulling it over a few minutes more, he decided that he *should* be pleased. Hadn't he intended to make her question her judgment? Wasn't that why he'd been so brutal with her? He'd known that facing the facts wouldn't be easy for her, and that making the decision to dump Logan would be a painstaking process for her. So why was he sitting there feeling guilty over upsetting her emotional equilibrium, when he was accomplishing his goal?

Why indeed? he thought. He should be delighted that she was brooding over her affair with Logan. And deep down, he decided, he probably was delighted, but somehow the elation was getting lost in the gut-wrenching guilt he was feeling over making her miserable.

In her office, Susan had pulled herself together enough to review the rest of the papers on today's shipments, and when she finished she had a new concern over the job. The video equipment she was to install to tape the stuffing of the crates was overdue. Remembering that another truck had arrived, she walked to Clark's office and tapped lightly on the open door.

His face brightened when he saw her. "Steffie. How's the headache?"

"A little better, but not much." After a pause, she said, "I haven't seen the paperwork on that last truckload. Was there anything in it from Optimal Optics?"

"No. It was just a few boxes from Noble Offshore. Replacement nuts and bolts, looked like. Nothing big. That's why I didn't bother you with the paperwork."

"No problem," Susan said. "Victor just keeps asking about the Optimal shipment. He's trying to diversify our client base so LIFT isn't so dependent on oil patch traffic, and he worked to get Optimal's business a long time. He promised their rep we'd treat this shipment with kid gloves, so it's on his mind. Would you let me know when it comes in so I can personally oversee it?"

"Sure."

Tiredly she brushed her forehead with her fingertips. "I think I'm going to take off early today. You can batten the hatches without me, can't you?"

"Sure. Steffie? Are you okay? Really?"

"I just need some aspirin and a nap." She left the warehouse with a feeling of having escaped—from the enormity of the job she'd undertaken and the hopelessness of the situation with Haggerty.

At the condo, she liberated Jezebel's kitten and the energetic ball of fluff followed her to the bathroom, bearing silent witness as Susan shed Steffie's gabardine suit with the relief of a knight discarding heavy mail after a joust, then put on clothes that were vintage Susan Carlson: soft faded jeans and an oversize knit jersey. Comfortable at last and intent on relaxing, Susan stretched out on the sofa with a book in her hand and the kitten curled up on her midsection.

Relax, she did, and then some. She wasn't even through the prologue of the book before she fell asleep. When the doorbell rang later, she jerked to wakefulness, startling the kitten, who skittered away in a dither. Susan had no concept of how much time had passed since she'd drifted off to sleep. Groggily she consulted the clock on the mantle: six-thirty. Her first coherent thought was that she'd been sleeping with her contact lenses in. The second was to wonder who was at the door. Peter would be home in suburbia by now, and she didn't know anyone else in town.

Except Clark Haggerty.

In one hand he held a brown paper grocery bag, in the other a stem of orchids surrounded by a spray of baby's breath. For several seconds, both of them were too disconcerted for speech, Susan by the shock of seeing him there and Clark by the sight of her in such starkly casual clothes with her hair ruffled, her feet bare and her eyes still slightly glazed by sleep. He wanted to take her in his arms and hug her; she looked so eminently huggable. And kissable. And... He suppressed a groan, and wondered if it was possible for a man to die of sexual frustration.

"Clark?" Her inflection emphasized the question mark after his name. He held up the bag self-consciously and explained, "I brought you some aspirin."

She eyed the grocery bag skeptically and said, "That's a mighty big bottle."

"I brought a bottle of wine, too, and—" he shrugged sheepishly "—well, they were a bright color, and I thought they might cheer you up."

She took the bundle of flowers and smiled. "Thank you. I love orchids. They're so exotic and rare."

"Like you," he said, and with a fluid economy of motion he stepped through the door, closed it behind him and slid his arms around her. Reflexively she jerked the hand with the fragile blossoms aside as he pulled her against him. Clark never even noticed. His lips found hers, claiming them urgently. The bottle of wine dropped to the floor and bounced on the thick carpet as both his hands caressed her lovingly.

Her body was warm and solid under the soft knit of her shirt, and he thought the world would collapse, or explode, if he couldn't go on holding her. Her arms were around him, hugging his waist, and the rightness of it reached his brain through the myriad sensations that tasting and touching her sparked.

For Susan, there was magic in his embrace, a magic that engulfed her, delicately cocooning her in a fog of awareness. His touch was an affirmation of her womanhood, a reminder that she was whole and alive and capable of needing a man.

This man. The thought wafted through her mind—unnecessarily, for she knew it was Clark she was responding to and not simply a masculine body. Savoring the delicious sensations he aroused in her, she leaned into the solidity of his body, hugging him fiercely, and matched the ardor in his kiss.

He stroked her with loving hands, adoring her with his touch. She swirled in a whirlwind of ecstasy as his fingers slipped under her shirt, kneaded the soft, sensitive flesh over her ribs and moved upward in search of her breast. She gasped at the intensity of the new intimacy, and Clark whispered, "Steffie."

The name, spoken as an endearment, encased Susan's spine in ice. How could she love him when he called her another woman's name? How could she let him love her when he didn't know who she was?

She pulled away from him, and he stared down at her, reeling from the betrayal of her abandonment. Unable to face the accusation in his eyes, she ducked her head and said, "We can't...." She sucked in a deep breath. "I just can't, Clark. It wouldn't be right."

He put his hands on the tops of her arms and squeezed them gently until she looked up at him. "Nothing could be as wrong as my not making love to you right now."

Squeezing her eyes shut against tears that begged to be released, she shook her head and said, "You don't understand."

"I understand what's happening between us, and that nothing else is important. I need you, Steffie."

She shrugged her shoulders from his grasp. "Something else *is* important. I can't ignore it, pretend—"

"You've been pretending," he said harshly. "Pretending your affair with Victor Logan is going to end happily ever after, when—"

"You don't understand anything," she said bitterly. "Not anything."

Her eyes held the panic of a cornered animal. He sighed raggedly and, needing to touch her, pressed the fingers of one hand to her cheek. "Maybe I do," he said resignedly. "Even if you wanted to break it off with Victor, you wouldn't want to do it when he's gravely ill. You'd wait until he was strong enough to bear up."

Susan released the breath she was holding. That explanation was one he could believe. And respect. And as much as she despised lying to him, even by not straightening out his misconception, she had to let him go on believing it.

"Now is not the time for us," she said, wondering if there ever could be a time for them. How badly she wanted to believe that there would be something left between them when she was Susan again. But it seemed hopeless. There was too much he would have to accept—a different woman, children.

A long, awkward silence yawned between them. "I don't want to leave you this way," he said finally. "If I promised not to make things difficult for you, could we—" he shrugged "—perhaps rescue the wine and share a cup? For goodwill?"

They reached for the bag simultaneously, and their hands touched as they picked it up. Susan drew hers away. "I need to get these orchids in water. Why don't you get the ice bucket from the bar to chill that in."

Clark picked up the bucket and followed her to the kitchen. "There's an icemaker in the freezer," she said as she filled a ceramic vase with water.

While he packed ice around the bottle of wine, she fussed with the flowers, arranging and rearranging them in the vase for the best effect. Finally she gave the baby's breath one last fluff and said, "Will you excuse me a moment?"

In the bathroom, she took out her contacts, put them in solution for a quick soak and blotted her face with a cool, damp cloth. Bracing her hands on the sides of the basin, she checked her makeup in the vanity mirror and groaned. What the episode at the warehouse hadn't undone, the unplanned nap and the scene with Clark had managed to ravage. Frowning because there wasn't time to redo from scratch, she did a hurried repair job and put her contacts back in.

The reflection of the sunken tub seemed to mock her as she made a final inspection of her repair efforts. Clark was so close—she had only to call him and she could live out her fantasy of sharing the bath with him.

Perhaps she should, she mused. Perhaps she should fill the tub and climb in and call him, then confront him with a seductive invitation to join her. She hadn't planned on falling in love, but since she had, maybe she should do this vastly selfish thing and snatch some romantic interludes to remember after she quit being Sensational Steffie and went back to being plain old Susie Cuke.

Steffie wouldn't have any qualms about inviting Clark into the tub for some underwater action, Susan thought bitterly. But she wasn't Steffie. God, how aware of that fact she was! Such a lapse would not only be unethical, it would be grossly unfair to Clark. He was going to feel foolish enough when he learned she'd been deceiving him. Intuition told her that if she compounded all the necessary lies with one final, intentional deception, the breach between them would be forever irreparable.

Spontaneously she picked up Steffie's perfume atomizer and sprayed the scent into the air, then walked through the flowers-and-musk mist on her way out of the room. Why shouldn't a jersey smell as sweet as a silk shirt? Women like Steffie Meeks had no exclusive franchise on smelling good.

She wasn't prepared for the sight that awaited her in the living room, and couldn't quite believe it. Clark was seated on the sofa with Jezebel's kitten in his lap. The cat was on its back with its feet in the air, swiping at Clark's fingers as he teased and tickled it playfully.

"Looks like you two have made friends," she said.

"It was her idea." He gently probed the cat's chest with a wiggling forefinger, and the kitten hissed and swatted at it. "She's still a little hellion."

"She likes to play," Susan said, sinking into a chair opposite the sofa. "I didn't know if she would, but she seems to enjoy being held and pampered."

One of the strokes of the tiny claws struck home, and Clark jerked his hand away with an indignant, "Ow!"

"Shall I hunt up some iodine?" she asked wryly.

He cast her a withering look before going back to fighting with the kitten. "I don't think the situation calls for first aid this time."

"You know," Susan said, "I don't care for wine on an empty stomach, and I don't have any cheese or crackers in the house. Why don't I fix us some dinner?"

"You weren't feeling well, and I was concerned," he said. "I didn't come to wangle a dinner invitation."

"It wouldn't be fancy," she warned. "I've got some chicken breasts in the freezer, and everything for tossed salad."

"If you're sure," Clark said, clearly wanting to stay, "but I insist on tossing the salad."

"Deal," she said.

The meal was casual, and they decided to finish off the bottle of wine on the small patio. Steffie apparently wasn't an outdoor person, because there were no lawn chairs, so they sat on throw cushions pilfered from a stack in the living room and leaned against the glass patio door while they sipped from crystal goblets.

Twilight dissolved into moonlight as they watched the sunset. Their conversation was punctuated with long, comfortable lapses of silence, and they spoke on random topics.

"There are no fireflies in the city," Susan said wistfully, staring out at distant streetlamps and traffic lights. "I used to chase fireflies when I was a little girl. I wanted to put them in a bottle to make a lantern, but I could never catch them, so I caught some of those ugly black lovebugs instead and got mad because they wouldn't shine."

She was still chasing fireflies that eluded her, Clark thought, still trying to make a lantern with bugs that didn't glow. In the muted light her delicate profile was crisp, her small, aristocratic nose perfect, her lips sensuous. She was a woman of such contrasts. There was none of the arrogant ice maiden in her tonight. Gingerly he stretched his arm across her shoulders and, when she rested her head in the crook of his shoulder, tightened it to caress the top of her arm.

They sat that way for almost an hour, silent and content, with the enchanted moonlight spilling over them and a gentle breeze wafting through their hair. At last Susan sighed languidly and snuggled closer to him. "I feel so divinely idle. Wine always makes me mellow."

Clark rested his chin on her temple. It was wonderfully, masculinely rough with a day's growth of beard. "It's not just the wine," he said.

She stretched her arm across his waist to hug him. "No. It's not."

Careful, Clark cautioned himself, *the wrong move, too much pressure now, and you'll lose her.* He kissed her temple lightly and whispered, "There could be other nights like this."

Susan wanted to believe him, but the clock was chasing them, nipping at their heels while their time ticked away. Six days. How many lazy nights could they steal in six days? How many memories could she squirrel away in less than a week?"

"You've got to leave now," she said, raising her head.

"I don't want to move."

"We both have to work tomorrow."

"You're always so damned practical," he said, reluctantly taking his arm from around her.

Susan stood and smoothed the denim of her jeans. "It comes with authority."

He stood, too, and they were just inches apart on the small balcony. "Thank you for dinner."

"Thank you for the wine. And the orchids."

He was studying her face as though memorizing her features, and she was unable to look away from him, to break contact with his probing, adoring brown eyes. After a long, long silence, he said, "I'll go stark raving mad if I don't kiss you good-night."

She slipped her arms around his waist and nestled her cheek against the solid wall of his chest. "They'd have to bring two straitjackets."

Chapter Eight

Clark, pouring water into the coffee maker, heard the downstairs door open and looked down from the loft landing as Susan entered the warehouse. Framed by the rectangle of sunshine in the doorway, her beauty took on an exquisite, ethereal quality, and her slender body, profiled by the light behind her, was lithe and womanly. He sensed, rather than saw, her smile as she waved at him.

Remembering the first time he'd seen her crossing that warehouse and how surprised he'd been to find himself attracted to her, he walked to the top of the stairs to wait for her and greeted her with a cheery, "Good morning."

There was a gleam in her vivid green eyes as she returned his greeting, and pride that he had put it

there welled in his chest. He didn't know where hi
relationship with her was headed, but he knew tha
what they shared was more than the passing infat
uation he had first perceived it to be, and he wa
more determined than ever after last night to per
suade her to sever her ties with Logan. He was sur
she was on the verge of that decision. Her kiss ha
confirmed it.

Unless she was playing him for a fool. He dis
missed that nagging doubt immediately. Steffie wa
incapable of that sort of manipulation. If she ha
been using him for a substitute while Logan was in
disposed, he would have been in her bed last nigh
instead of sitting on her patio looking at the stars.

On the way to the warehouse, Susan had won
dered if the moonlit interlude the night before ha
been a dream. In the face of the bright morning su
the special intimacy between them had seemed to
magical to be trusted, but now, as she basked in th
warmth of this open, friendly smile, she knew tha
intimacy had been, and still was, genuine. She wa
acutely aware of his physical presence close to her a
she stepped onto the small loft landing. He was
virile man, large and strong, and she felt if sh
touched him, she might absorb some of his strengtl
and the quiet confidence his strength exuded. *Oh
Lord, where was she going to get the strength to fac
him when he learned how she'd deceived him?*

Clark watched the gleam fade from her eyes, to b
replaced by an ominous cloud of emotion. Was sh
thinking of Logan? he wondered. Having pangs o

guilt over her attraction to another man? Sometimes he thought there must be something else that haunted her, something that sparked a brooding turbulence inside her. He wanted to hold her and ask her what it was. He couldn't imagine anything so awful that they couldn't face it together.

Unable to resist the urge to touch her, he brushed her elbow with his fingertips, and when she looked up at him, he said, "Did you sleep well last night?"

Her eyes met his evenly. "Wine always makes me sleepy."

His voice grew husky. "Home cooking does it for me."

A blush spread over Susan's face, warming it. The words they used were so irrelevant, the communication between them so explicit. They shared a rapport that either existed between two people immediately or never existed at all, an invisible, intangible bonding of their minds.

It had been that way with Greg, too, right from the start. She hadn't thought it possible that it could be that way with anyone else, that she could meet two men in a lifetime with whom she could feel this oneness of spirit.

Life had been good with Greg. She knew instinctively that it could be good with Clark. *If.* God, how that word plagued her. If he could forgive her deceptions; if he could accept who and what she was.

Clark interrupted her train of thought. "Coffee's brewed. Care for a cup?"

"Talked me into it," she answered. "I could use something to get me going."

I could think of things a lot more exciting than coffee to get you going, Miss Meeks, Clark thought, but refrained from saying it aloud. "Cream or sugar?" he asked.

"A bit of both."

They didn't linger on the landing but, as if by mutual consent, carried their cups of coffee into their respective offices. Susan had nothing to do except skim over the paperwork from the small shipment that had arrived the previous afternoon. After initialing it and tossing it into the out basket, she opened the top drawer of Victor's desk and took out the envelope she'd found the previous week. Season tickets for two for a musical theater series at the Music Hall. There was a performance tomorrow night, and Logan had okayed her using them. Even though she'd hoped to take in some live theater while in Houston, she had given up on going because she wasn't gutsy enough to go running around downtown on a Saturday night by herself.

Tyler had originally volunteered to drive up from Brownsville and take her out on the town, but Susan nixed the idea of calling him as soon as she thought of it. He believed she was in Houston for a training seminar of some sort, and even if she wore one of her own dresses and kept him away from the condo, she'd be hard pressed to explain her hairstyle. She laughed softly at the thought of conservative-to-the-bone Tyler's reaction to apricot fizz, but she sobered quickly.

Poor Tyler. If she called him now, she'd be using him, and they'd been taking advantage of each other for too long already. The next time she saw him she wanted to level with him about the hopelessness of their relationship, and a Broadway musical wasn't an appropriate preamble to a heart-to-heart like that.

She read the tickets again. Tomorrow's date, 8:00 p.m., *My Fair Lady*. She'd never seen a major production of a musical. It could be a special evening—very special indeed if she saw it with Clark.

No guts, no glory, she told herself. What did she have to lose by asking him? If he said no, he said no. And if he said yes—

The buzzing of her intercom rudely tore into her fantasy. "Steffie Meeks," she said into the receiver.

"That shipment from Optimal Optics is here," Clark's voice informed her with a note of petulance. "You said you wanted to personally supervise it."

"I'll be right down."

It was steamy and warm near the open bay door on the loading dock. About a dozen palleted crates, just off-loaded, were on the concrete platform, waiting to be forklifted to a storage area. Clark waved from where he was standing in the rear of the delivery van, and she walked to the edge of the dock. "This is it," he said, patting a chest-high wooden crate. "Where do you want it?"

"I thought over there, next to the wall."

He ran the back of one hand across his sweaty forehead. "In the temporary holding area?"

Nodding, she said, "I want it in plain sight where I can keep an eye on it. Victor's orders."

He shrugged. "I never argue with the boss." Using a dolly, he moved the crate himself and, under her anxious supervision, put it exactly where she wanted it.

Susan was impressed by how unobtrusive, how extraordinarily ordinary the crate appeared. Not even the shrewdest, most suspicious observer would give it more than a cursory perusal. Tonight, after everyone else had left the warehouse, she would hook up the equipment the way Peter had shown her and test it, but that was later. At the moment, she had some personal business to attend to. "Are you about finished down here?" she asked Clark.

"Until another truck comes in."

"There's something I'd like to talk to you about when you have a minute."

Sensing that she wanted to talk about something that wasn't related to business, he cocked an eyebrow suggestively and said, "Your office or mine?"

"Mine," she said, lowering her eyes, suddenly shy. They walked together up the stairs, and when they were seated, she laid the tickets on the desk between them. "LIFT is a season subscriber to Theatre Under the Stars. These tickets are for tomorrow. I know it's short notice, but I thought that you...that we...if you wanted to..."

Clark picked up the tickets, skimmed the information on them, then replaced them on the desk. He'd been planning on spending most of Saturday night at the library, studying. "I'd like to go with you to the Music Hall," he said, and his eyes spoke of more intimate desires as they fixed on her face.

Color rose high in her cheeks, burning them. "Good," she said hoarsely. "It's a date."

He almost had her, Clark thought. Encouraged by her willingness to be seen with him in a highly visible public place, he was more sure than ever that she was close to being ready to break off her relationship with Logan. "We'll go to dinner first," he said, and she nodded.

Jumping frijoles, this place was spooky at night, Susan thought with considerable trepidation. Except for the watchman walking rounds outside, she was the only person on the premises, and strategically placed security lights cast irregular circles of illumination that produced eerie shadows. The tattoo of her footsteps echoed in the cavernous dock area, breaking through the ominous, overpowering silence. Susan found it oddly reassuring, a rhythm like the beating of a heart that proved one was alive.

She switched on only one light, the one closest to the crate containing the video equipment, before going to work, performing step by step the procedures Peter had drilled into her memory. She realized now the merit of his training-by-rote methods. The ease with which she opened the crate and pre-

pared the camera for operation astounded her and
replenished her waning store of confidence. Her
hands were steady, her mind sharp, as she removed
protective foam pads and lens caps and checked dials
and switches and the viewfinder. Finally she un-
rolled the cord, plugged it into the socket behind the
wall and switched on the camera.

After turning on an additional row of lights, she
danced around in the camera's field of vision, recit-
ing "Mary Had a Little Lamb" with great emotional involvement.

Peter guffawed when he saw the test tape the next
morning. "The camera's functioning fine, but the
critics will cut you to ribbons," he teased.

"Eeets arrrt," she said, feigning a generic foreign
accent. "Vat do I keer vat the critics sez?"

Peter studied her quizzically. "Are you really as
cool about this as you're acting, or is all this calm a
form of hysteria?"

She exhaled heavily, feeling her energy drain from
her body along with the air from her lungs. "I've got
enough butterflies in my stomach to populate a
national forest."

"Good. Then you'll be on your toes. Compla-
cency is a dangerous thing in an agent."

An agent. God, was he really talking about her,
Susan Carlson? An agent? Was she really going to
help two criminals pack U.S. currency into pipes so
it could be smuggled out of the country—and videotape them as they performed the dastardly deed?
Smile for the camera, boys, you're facing twenty

years in the pen. The whole idea was ludicrous. And
dangerous. She'd been so preoccupied with Clark
Haggerty she'd almost lost sight of the precarious-
ness of the job ahead of her. It was going to require
every ounce of concentration she could bring to it.

She left Peter's office in a sober frame of mind.
She owed it to the Task Force and her own safety to
give her total concentration to the job she'd accepted, and she would when the time came. But there
was nothing she could do about the job until
Wednesday, so she intended to spend the weekend
thoroughly enjoying the "perks" Peter had de-
scribed when talking her into the job in the first
place.

Saturday. She was in a world-class city, and she
had a date to be wined and dined and taken to the
theater by a splendid man. She launched her afternoon of indulgence by going to the beauty shop for
a facial, a manicure and a shampoo and style.

Susan had given up wearing white the first time
Greg Junior had wiped strained-carrot-filled fingers
on her best blouse, so she had been waiting for the
right opportunity to wear the elegant white dress
she'd discovered in Steffie's closet. Tissue-paper
frail, the delicate fabric draped beautifully even on
the padded clothes hanger, and the skirt was full and
softly gathered. Thin black stripes, no thicker than
a piece of paper, shot vertically through the almost
luminescent silver-white silk at half-inch intervals,
lending it a note of crisp formality. She selected the

understatement of a strand of pearls at the neckline, and a wide bangle with black-and-white mother-of-pearl veneer for her wrist.

As accustomed as she had become to the precise styling and the arresting color of her hair, she still did a double take at the strange woman in the hall mirror as she answered Clark's ring of the doorbell. Pausing only briefly to eye the glamorous stranger, she knew that the change in her was not exclusively cosmetic. It was more than just a little pampering, an elegant dress, a fancy hairstyle. There was a change in attitude, something internal that shone through the glittering facade: the glow of a woman who'd cast aside the dull cloak of widowhood and fallen in love.

Any doubts she'd had about the depth or genuineness of her feelings evaporated as she covered the distance to the door and opened it to the warm reception of Clark's instantaneous smile. For the first time, she began to hope that there might be a chance for them, that the feelings that had developed between them might be strong enough to survive the inevitable shocks ahead of them. She had to hope; the idea that their relationship might end in a fog of bitterness was unthinkable.

The beginning of the evening passed with a bittersweet, dreamlike perfection. They ate in the revolving restaurant atop the Hyatt Hotel, more entranced by each other than by the view of downtown. Later, as they approached the Music Hall, she was struck by the elegance of the crowd assembled within the high glass walls of the foyer and realized that she, in Steffie's white dress, and Clark, in his dark suit, would fit right in. He wore a suit with surprising aplomb for such a starkly physical man. In fact, he seemed quite at home in a coat and tie.

Eschewing the wine and mixed drinks offered at the bar, they meandered their way through the crowded lobby. A short line had formed at the entrance to their section, where the ticket taker was carefully reading each ticket before lethargically tearing it in half. Clark's arm was across Susan's back, his hand resting lightly on her waist. Susan was so absorbed in his company that she didn't react to a feminine voice calling, "Steffie," until a finger tapped her shoulder and the name was repeated.

Swallowing the lump of panic in her throat, she forced herself to return the woman's smile.

The woman, a tall, slinky blonde in her early twenties, said, "Knew it had to be you when I saw your hair, and then I thought, of course, you must be using Victor's tickets. How is Victor, anyway?"

"He's recovering, but it's slow progress," Susan answered. "He may be going home next week."

The woman dismissed Victor's illness with a benign, "I'm sure he'll be more comfortable there." With renewed enthusiasm, she said, "You've got to meet Paul," and, tugging at her escort's arm, added, "Paul, this is Steffie Meeks, and..."

"Clark Haggerty," Clark supplied, shaking the hand she extended. In the melee and how-do-you-dos that followed, Susan learned that the woman's name was Diana. Thank God she at least had that much information.

A silence fell over the foursome temporarily after the introductions were accomplished, but Diana obviously wasn't a person at loss for words long. "Paul is my significant other," she announced, punctuating the statement with a lift of eyebrow that said she'd be interested in knowing more about Steffie's relationship with this Haggerty fellow.

Wishing the woman would go away and quit spoiling her evening, Susan replied, "How nice."

"Would you two care for a drink?" Paul invited graciously. "There's time before curtain."

Susan looked at Clark and held her breath, hoping he would perceive her reluctance. In a single expression, he told her silently, *I understand. I agree.* "We just came from dinner," he said.

"Then you're not going to Harvey's after the show?" Diana said as though discussing a crisis of major world importance.

Again furtive, communicative glances were exchanged. This time Susan answered. "Not tonight."

"Too bad," Diana said without conviction. "Well, nice seeing you, Steffie. I'll be sure and tell Daddy I ran into you. He's been concerned about Victor, and he'll be glad to hear he's recovering. Now you give Victor a big hug and tell him we all love him."

"I know he'll be glad to know you're thinking of him," Susan said, wondering about the link between this woman's father and Victor Logan.

"Call me sometime, and we'll go shopping or something," Diana said, and Susan nodded.

Relief poured over her as the couple walked away. While Diana apparently could hardly wait to rat on Steffie for two-timing Logan, she obviously hadn't suspected that Susan wasn't Steffie Meeks.

"While the cat's away..." Clark said under his breath.

"I beg your pardon," Susan said, looking up at him.

"That's what she's thinking," Clark said gravely. "While the cat's away, the mice will..."

In no mood to fight, Susan grinned. "I daresay she'd sacrifice two toes and a finger to know who you are and what's going on between us."

Clark's attitude had turned somber at the first mention of Logan's name, and he wasn't ready to be lifted out of the doldrums by a light phrase and a cocky grin. He cupped her elbow in his hand and propelled her forward as the line moved. "There's not nearly as much going on between us as I'd like," he said from behind clenched teeth.

Or I, Susan thought dolorously.

An usher handed them programs and escorted them to their seats. The familiar squeaks and groans of instruments being tuned sounded from the orchestra pit a few yards in front of them, and the ceiling of the hall hovered above them, high as the sky. Susan relaxed against the padded back of her seat, silently absorbing the ambience of the substantial building. Though not as opulent or ornate as the halls of earlier periods, rather plain and geometric, actually, the hall was impressive in its sheer size.

Clark was still brooding over the reminder that the woman he was with, in the eyes of those who knew her, was Logan's woman. What a damnable, cock-eyed situation! Logan had it all—wife, family, so-cial standing—yet when his mistress showed up in public with another man, eyebrows flew up in out-raged censure.

And Steffie…he thought, catching a whiff of her perfume as he admired the perfection of her profile. The little vixen! She had the gall to find amusement in that censure.

Dammit, he wasn't going to go on playing the fool opposite her vamp! Didn't she realize he loved her?

His mind reeled at the significance of what he'd just thought. His feelings had gone beyond infatua-tion but, good grief, did he *love* her—the long, last-ing, commitment type of love? As novel as the idea was to him, how was she supposed to know? He tumbled the possibility over in his mind again and again. Love was so . . . serious, so catalytic. The re-percussions of being in love with Steffie Meeks would certainly be cataclysmic. Was he ready for that kind of upheaval in his life, to be "in love"?

The chimes announcing curtain rang melodically, and the seats around them filled up. The house lights went down, the audience was welcomed by a repre-sentative from Theatre Under the Stars, the orches-tra burst into the lilting overture and the curtain went up.

Clark sought Steffie's hand, found it, closed his hand around it possessively and squeezed lightly.

Susan sensed Clark's preoccupation on the drive back to the condo and realized that it dated from the moment Logan's name had been mentioned. She purposefully didn't ask him about it. The evening had been nearly perfect until darling Diana had shown up, and Susan didn't want to sully it further by risking a shattering confrontation. So much of the evening had been special and sweet; she didn't want a bitter argument to spoil it.

But his brooding silence and the tight set of his jaw, unmistakable symptoms of a building tension, sparked a rising apprehension in Susan. She waited for him to broach the subject of Logan, waited with all the eager expectation of an errant child about to be lectured by the school principal.

It wasn't until they had arrived at the condo and Clark had turned off the engine of his small truck that the dam of restraint broke. Staring ahead through the windshield in his posture of resignation, his arm draped limply over the steering wheel, he said, "I can take you out in public, Steffie."

She poised her mouth to speak, then closed it, not knowing what to say. After an awkward pause, he cocked his then closed it, not knowing what to say. After an awkward pause, he cocked his head to look directly into her face and continued, "I couldn't give you a Corvette or an executive job with an expense account, but I can take you out in public without having to worry about my wife finding out or some-one mentioning it to my kids.''

"Clark," she pleaded.

Abruptly he grabbed the door handle and opened the door on his side of the car. "Let's go inside. This isn't the place for us to be talking."

As they walked to the condo, Susan moved as if her feet were lead weights. She didn't want to lie to him anymore, or even perpetuate the deception she'd already begun, but she had no choice. There was a grim determination in his gait that told her he wouldn't be dismissed at the door. Haggerty was gearing up for a confrontation as much as she was regretting the inevitability of one.

She tried. At the door, key in hand, she said, "It was a lovely evening, Clark. Very special. Thank you for going with me, and for dinner."

"It's not going to work," he said bluntly. "You're not going to dismiss me with a prissy little thank-you and send me away."

She exhaled in exasperation. "It's late, Clark."

"Not that late." He took the key from her hand, unlocked the door and gestured for her to go in. He followed closely behind her. She stopped in the mid-dle of the room, without turning to face him, and shuddered when he put his hand on her shoulder. "It's time to talk about Logan," he said.

"The man is ill," she lied—convincingly because of the intensity of emotion in her voice. "It's wrong—"

"Then let's talk about us instead."

"Now's not the time," she argued feebly, futilely.

One step brought him so close to her that she could feel the heat of his body behind her. When he wrapped his arms around her shoulders, she sighed, closed her eyes and relaxed against him, relishing the warm, masculine hardness of his chest against her shoulder blades. "Now *is* the time," he said, nuzzling his smooth-shaven cheek against hers and tightening the circle of his arms, hugging her closer.

Nothing they could have said, not even the most carefully chosen words of a poet, would have defined their feelings as explicitly as the silent communication in their touch. Susan could have been content to remain in his arms forever, bathing in the magic of being next to him and knowing that he cared for her.

But Clark refused to be dissuaded. "You know what's going on between us, Steffie. You feel it, too. I *feel* you feeling it. You couldn't feel that way with me if you truly loved Logan."

He gave her the opportunity to respond, to deny or argue or agree, but she said nothing. She was so silent and so still that, except for her softness and warmth and the floral musk of her perfume, she might have been a lifeless statue in his arms.

"I'm sure you're fond of him, Steffie," he continued, "and you're loyal. You don't want to hurt him, betray him. I understand that. But don't you see that if you don't break free of him he'll destroy you? He gives you *things* Steffie, and he probably says he loves you, but don't you see that if he loved you he wouldn't hold you prisoner in this kind of social cell? He couldn't take you to the Music Hall and hold your hand. *I* can." Gently he turned her in his arms so that they faced each other. His final, emphatic "*I* can," was spoken by lips en route to hers, and the pronouncement was sealed with a kiss, urgent, deep and demanding.

An eternity later he loosened his hold on her and, still encircling her waist with one arm, raised the opposite hand to cradle her cheek and guide her face toward his. He said the name again, as an endearment, the only name he associated with her: "Steffie."

Tears clouded her eyes. Would he ever say "Susan" with that same cherishing inflection? Could he cherish Susan with the intensity she could see so plainly in the depths of his brown eyes as they locked with hers?

His voice was a sensuous, persuasive whisper. "Tell me you care, Steffie. Admit it. Tell me you'll break free of Logan so we'll have a chance together."

A small, pitiful noise came from somewhere in her throat, a miserable wail of frustration and unshed tears. Clark thought his heart would burst with loving her as he waited for her to form the cry into speech.

"Logan..." she began, and was unable to continue. Still, he waited, unable and unwilling to give up before he had extracted a promise, a commitment of some kind from her. She sucked in a deep, ragged breath. "In a week Logan won't be between us anymore. I can promise you that much."

Weak with relief, he sighed heavily and pulled her to him, wrapping his arms around her, encasing her, protecting her. "You won't be sorry, Steffie. I'll never make you sorry."

Another eternity passed while he held her. Safe, content in his arms but knowing she couldn't remain there, Susan burrowed her cheek against his chest and savored the sweetness for as long as it lasted.

Clark ended it with a kiss that began tenderly but became demanding and, ultimately, posed the question to which the answer had to be no. The question, though explicit, required no words for the asking, but the explicit answer was firmly spoken as she reluctantly pulled away from him. "Not now, Clark. Not tonight. It wouldn't be fair."

To either of us, her mind completed, *but especially to you.*

Stunned by the refusal, he stared at her in disbelief for several seconds before saying, "All right, Steffie. If you want to talk to Logan before we...get involved, I'll respect that. I guess..."

Her fingertips were soft against the roughness of his male cheek as she caressed it. "How did you get this scar?"

His voice was expressionless. "Playing cowboys and Indians when I was ten. I fell off a roof."

On tiptoe she kissed the faint triangle. "It has to be this way," she assured him. "There's no choice."

He covered her hand with his. Turning it, he kissed the inside of her palm. He felt her shudder as she sighed. "Leaving you feels so wrong," he said.

She couldn't remember a single moment in her life when she had been so torn by a decision—or had so bitterly regretted making the right choice. Stepping back into the precious, comforting circle of his arms, she said, "Hold me for a while first."

Chapter Nine

Cruz called midmorning on Monday. His voice was deep, and he spoke excellent English, somewhat stiffly, with just a trace of a Spanish accent. "I understand you're filling in for Mr. Logan while he's ill."

"That's correct," Susan said.

"There is a shipment at your warehouse that interests me."

"I understand. I know which shipment."

"I should like to inspect that shipment."

"That can be arranged."

"This would require—" he paused for effect "—a certain amount of discretion. As I recall, your warehouse is closed on Wednesday afternoons. Perhaps I could inspect that shipment at one o'clock on Wednesday?''

"That would be ideal, Señor Cruz."

"I shall meet you then, Miss Logan."

After hanging up the receiver, Susan pulled a tissue from the box she'd stashed in the bottom desk drawer and wiped her sweaty palm. The equipment was set up, the rendezvous set. All she had to worry about were the hyperactive butterflies that had taken up residence in the pit of her stomach. She'd handled crisis situations on the bridge, but they were always impromptu, a quick reaction to some unexpected circumstance. This gut-tingling anticipation was different, worse by far than the shock of realizing afterward what *might* have happened.

Absently massaging an eyebrow with her fingertips, Susan reflected that she might be coping with the stress of the assignment better if her love life weren't dangling precariously on a gossamer thread spun of hopes and wishes. It was so nerve-racking being close to Clark, needing him, knowing he had faith in the falsehoods he believed about her, and not knowing how he would react when his faith was shaken. Would he be able to separate the truth of their love from the extraneous falsehoods that surrounded it—was it even reasonable to expect such extraordinary tolerance and understanding?

Powerless to settle anything with him until her job was done, she forced herself to concentrate on the details that would minimize risk during her meeting with Cruz. Ironically Clark was her biggest concern.

Shrewd, intelligent, he was an omniscient foreman, alert to anything out of the ordinary in the warehouse. If he became suspicious or curious, he would be like a hound after a hare, trying to find out what was going on. And his interference could be catastrophic, potentially fatal. The boys they were playing with weren't the homespun, fun-loving crowd from the neighborhood playground. They would play for keeps if they found themselves compromised or backed into a corner. Clark Haggerty—and Susan Carlson, too, for that matter—could disappear from the face of the earth if these boys suspected a trap.

She met with Peter and Logan at the hospital to devise a surefire plan to get Clark away from the warehouse early on Wednesday. Logan suggested they set up an appointment with one of LIFT's consulting accountants for a review of the current LIFT rates.

"There probably won't be any recommendations for changes, so it'll be a routine session, but it should keep Clark occupied for an hour or so," he said, "and the accountant's office is at least half an hour from the warehouse, which'll buy you more time."

He set it up with a phone call, thanking the accountant for the inquiries into his health, assuring him that he was recovering nicely, explaining that he and Steffie would be unavailable for this quarterly meeting and that he was sending his new warehouse foreman as his official representative.

Once past the shock of having been caught in the middle of something that could send him to prison for a very long time, Logan, hoping for lenient treatment in the courts, had been a study in cooperation. The expression on his face as he hung up the phone was smug and showed a glimmer of excitement, as though, once drawn into it, he was enjoying being in on the intrigue. "It's set for ten-thirty Wednesday. By the time he's done, it'll be too late to come back to the warehouse. It'll be closed already."

Susan waited until Wednesday morning to spring the meeting on Clark. As usual, they chatted on the landing a few minutes before going to work, and she waited until they were about to adjourn to their offices before she said offhandedly, "Come on into my office for a minute or two. I just remembered something."

He listened solemnly while she explained about the meeting with the accountant. "Victor thinks this would be an excellent opportunity for you to get a feel for the pricing policy." She had written the accountant's name and office address on her notepad, and she tore the page from the pad and slid it across the desk. "You might as well call it a day when you're finished there. I'll be here to close up, and you can brief me in the morning."

She wondered, because of the way he was looking at her, if he sensed her anxiety. He poised his mouth to speak, reconsidered, then, picking up the paper, said, "Whatever Victor wants."

Watching him stalk out of her office, she wanted to cry out for him to come back. On the eve of her meeting with criminals, she needed his support, his strength, the comforting reassurance of his touch. Involuntarily she said his name aloud. He stopped, turned and looked at her questioningly. His posture was one of preparedness, and she knew instinctively that she only had to gesture and he would rush across the room, hug her and whisper reassurances in her ear. He would give her his strength without knowing or asking why she needed it, and because he would share it so unselfishly, she couldn't take advantage of him by asking for it.

"Don't forget to keep track of your mileage."

It was the most asinine remark she'd ever uttered in her life; the emptiness of it left them both feeling hollow.

Later, perhaps half an hour, she heard him calling her, a crisp, professional summons, and followed the direction of his voice to the storage room. No sooner had she passed through the door than it was shoved closed behind her and she was gathered into Clark's arms and clutched there with an urgency that was almost alarming. He lowered his lips over hers and kissed her hungrily, as though he needed her for the sustenance of life and had been starving for her.

When his lips left hers, he still held her anchored against him with one arm across her waist, the fingers of his other hand threaded through her hair, cupping her scalp and pressing her head against his chest. "You didn't break it off with Logan," he said with raw anguish in his voice that tore into her heart. "You saw him and talked to him, but you didn't tell him."

Susan wanted to say something to soothe his hurt, but only the truth could comfort him, and it would be hours before she could give him that. She sighed heavily against his chest, a sigh of pain and resignation, and said his name raggedly.

He released her abruptly, but only long enough to move his hands to the curve of her shoulders. He squeezed them firmly but not punishingly and put his face inches from hers to demand her attention. "Let's tell him, Steffie. Together. Now. Come with me to the hospital. I know he's sick, but if he's strong enough to issue directives, he can take it. He's got a wife to comfort him."

All that would come out of Susan's parched throat was a broken half cry.

Clark refused to give up. "Please, Steffie," he pleaded. "Let's go. Now. Before..." His voice trailed off, and with an exhausted sigh, he released her.

She reached up to cradle his cheeks in her hand. There was a liquid quality in her voice, as though it were strained through tears. "Oh, Clark, please believe me when I tell you that you don't have to worry about Logan coming between us."

His hands covered hers, and he drew her right palm to his lips and kissed it. "Would you...if I told you..."

The ensuing silence was still and empty as death as she waited for him to finish. He didn't, and she prompted expectantly, "If you told me?"

His eyes fixed on her face, and he stared at her for a very long time. His hands fell away from hers; his arms hung limply at his sides. "Now's not the time," he said, turning her own phrase against her.

She thought, when he walked away, that the droop of his shoulders appeared as forlorn as she felt at that moment, but she changed her mind. Nothing could appear quite that forlorn.

On his way to the meeting, he stopped at the door to her office. "I'm leaving now."

She nodded gravely, and they stared at each other for a moment. There was a sadness in his eyes that echoed her own frustration, and the mouth that so often was touched by a smile was fixed in a hard, grim line. He seemed loath to leave, as though he were afraid that if he left he might never see her again, and his footsteps were sluggish and heavy on the concrete stairs, almost as though he knew something ominous and significant was about to come between them.

Susan shrugged away the possibility. There was no way he could know about her or the operation that was about to come to a head. She'd covered her tracks too well. He must be picking up on her anxiety and reflecting it in his impatience over Steffie's ties with Logan.

Time dragged as she waited for the warehouse to close, shuffling papers and watching the hands on the office clock creep lethargically toward the twelve. She fell victim to the "don't think" phenomenon: the more she tried not to think about meeting Cruz, the more firmly fixed her mind became on the encounter ahead. Stage fright was too mild a term for the anticipation that turned her insides into a quivering mass.

She felt she'd aged fifty years by high noon, when the hubbub of activity on the loading dock ceased and the cavernous warehouse took on the echoing stillness of a crypt. The security guard, a retired marine sergeant named Mickey, made his rounds, checking doors and bays, and mounted the steps to the landing. Susan looked up from the papers she'd spread on her desk.

"Mr. Haggerty gone already?" he asked, poking his head in her doorway.

"He had a meeting, so I'm holding down the fort," Susan answered.

"You gonna work long?"

She swept a hand in the air over the papers and shrugged.

"Well, I'll keep an extra careful watch out if you're going to be here by yourself."

"Thanks, Mickey." She let him get almost to the stairs before she said, "Oh, Mickey, there's a Mr. Cruz and an associate coming at one. Please let them in the employee entrance."

Mickey granted her the indulgent smile of a male chauvinist humoring a "little woman." "Glad you told me, Miz Meeks. I'd have told them to come back during business hours tomorrow.''

Which is why I told you, she thought crossly. God, she was on edge, impatient now for Mickey to leave so she could hook up the video equipment and get the Colombian shipment into place within range of its lens.

The camera took only seconds to activate and, after three trips with the dolly, she had the boxes in position. Another interminable twenty-five minutes crept past before Cruz arrived.

From the loft landing where she waited for him, her first impression of Cruz was of sleekness. From his immaculately groomed raven hair to his top-of-the-line patent lace-ups, Cruz projected an aura of high fashion backed by big bucks.

The harvest of crime, Susan thought bitterly. As he had on the phone, he spoke with clipped, proper English tinged with a trace of his native Spanish. "It is always a pleasure to meet so lovely a woman," he said, shaking the hand she extended upon reaching the base of the stairs. Susan had to force the smile with which she accepted the brazen appraisal that accompanied the compliment.

Ramón Cantu was less suave than his companion. His stocky, muscular body didn't lend itself as much to the fashion-mannequin look, and his grunted greeting was far removed from Cruz's polished speech.

Obviously the muscle man, Susan thought. *Cruz's flunky, henchman and bodyguard.* He was carrying two leather valises, each about triple the size of the standard briefcase Cruz held in his left hand.

"The shipment you were interested in is over here, Señor Cruz," Susan said, leading him toward the boxes.

Cruz read the shipping label on the most convenient box and nodded. "Very good. Yes. This is the proper shipment. Cantu..."

Automatically Cantu stepped forward and popped the flaps of the box apart, revealing a large metal elbow pipe about a foot in diameter and partly buried in foam shipping chips. Cantu looked from the pipe to Cruz and, getting a go-ahead nod, reached down into the chips to lift out the pipe joint.

My God, Susan thought, *they're like cartoon caricatures.* Except, of course, they were real criminals.

Cantu was still holding the pipe joint when the sound of a key working the lock in the metal door momentarily froze them. Cruz was the first to appraise the situation and react. With a jerk of his head toward a tall wooden crate, he directed Susan and Cantu behind it, out of view of anyone entering the door.

"Who?" Cruz asked, somehow making the softly spoken inquiry a threat. Susan, in a heightened state of awareness, noted from the corner of her eye that Cantu had scooted the valises across the floor so that they were at his feet. His hand was inside his coat in the general area that a shoulder-holstered gun would be.

She shook her head in reply to Cruz's question, denying knowledge of who might be intruding. "The security guard, perhaps," she suggested lamely, "making sure the door is secure."

A menacing glint glowed in Cruz's eye. "It was a key turning, Miss Meeks," he spat, "not a watchman's rattle."

A creak accompanied a flood of sunlight as the door opened. Reflexively they shrank farther back behind the crate. Susan felt Cruz tense beside her. She wasn't sure at what point she'd begun holding her breath.

"Steffie."

It was Clark's voice. Susan's scalp prickled. Cantu's hand was still in his coat, poised. *Oh, God, don't let them hurt him.*

Cruz looked at her questioningly. Susan exhaled the breath she'd been holding and whispered, as evenly as possible, "It's okay. It's our foreman. I can get rid of him."

"I hope so," Cruz whispered, his voice dripping with menace.

On legs made of limp noodles, hoping she didn't faint dead away from fear, Susan stepped out from behind the crate and walked toward Clark. "I thought you were gone for the day, Clark." Did her voice sound normal? She couldn't tell.

"I thought I'd pick up the papers from this morning's shipments and go over them tonight. I didn't expect to find you here, but I saw the Corvette."

Was she hypersensitive, or was he skimming the storage area curiously?

"There was a strange car outside. I thought someone might be here," he continued.

"Mickey probably parked on this side of the building."

"Maybe we should check what we're paying him. It was a pretty fancy car for a night watchman."

"Probably his son's. He leaves it with Mickey when he's out of the country."

Clark didn't look entirely convinced, but he dropped the subject. "What are you doing here so late?"

"Waiting on a phone call."

"Down here?"

The conversation was beginning to take on the overtones of an inquisition. "I noticed Jezebel sitting on that stack of boxes—" she pointed to the opposite side of the room from where Cruz and Cantu were hiding "—and I thought I might be able to talk my way up to her and get her to let me pet her." Did this sudden gift of fabrication spring from desperation?

"Did she let you?"

"She took off when the door opened."

"You chased her?"

"I lost her behind that crate." Damn his penchant for observing every little thing that went on! She could imagine Cruz getting tenser, Cantu's hand closing around his gun nervously. Clark *had* to leave.

They had reached the bottom of the stairs, and
Clark put his hand on the small of her back com-
panionably. Oh, God, what if he decided to kiss her?
He'd know something was wrong. She couldn't put
her heart, or any other part of her anatomy, into
kissing him, knowing that Cantu's hand was posed
over a gun.

"Why don't I go over the paperwork while you're
waiting on your call, then I'll take you out for some
lunch?"

Susan gasped. "I . . . I'm not hungry."

"You didn't have lunch, did you?"

"I had a candy bar from the machine—"

"That's not enough."

"And I have some errands to run this afternoon."

They stepped onto the landing. He looked at her
strangely. "Are you all right, Steffie?"

No! she wanted to shout. *I'm not okay. There's a
man downstairs with a gun, and he might shoot the
two of us if you don't get out of here.* "Sure," she
said, affecting the flippancy she'd developed for her
Steffie persona. "Why?"

"You seem . . . tense, and if I didn't know better,
I'd think you were trying to get rid of me."

Oh, you poor, perceptive, adorable boob! "I, uh,
I am, Clark. It's . . ." She paused uncomfortably,
licking dry lips. "It's Victor who's supposed to call,
and I . . ." Another uncomfortable hesitation and an
indrawn fortifying breath. "It's so awkward talking

with him now, knowing what I have to tell him, and I wouldn't feel comfortable with you here."

Quite an impressive lie, she congratulated herself, and, noting the hard set of his mouth, realized it had pushed the right button. She knew his point of vulnerability.

With a peculiar, sad expression in his eyes, he said, "All right, Steffie. I'll leave."

Tension that had been coiled in her chest like a compressed spring eased. Thank goodness. She stood in the doorway to her office, biting her bottom lip, while he fetched the papers from his desk.

Pausing briefly on his way back to the stairs, he glowered at her and said sharply, "Tell Victor hello for me."

She waited until he was out the door, then ran downstairs. Cruz and Cantu crept out from behind the crate. "I'm sorry," she said, "He wasn't supposed to be here."

"It's fortunate that he left without seeing us," Cruz said significantly.

There were no more interruptions. Cantu lifted the pipe joint from the box again, and Cruz opened one of the satchels. Although she'd known what was inside, Susan gasped involuntarily at the sight of so much money—U.S. currency in fifty- and hundred-dollar bills, all neatly bound into bundles.

Cruz laughed at her reaction. "It is lovely, isn't it? In its own way, it is as lovely as a woman...although not nearly as soft or warm." His eyes grazed boldly, lecherously, over her face and down to the curve of

her breast under the fabric of her dress. Susan felt
sullied by the perusal.

"How much is there this time?" she asked for the
benefit of the video camera.

"In all, a million and a half," Cruz said.

The men jammed a dozen and a half, perhaps two
dozen bundles into the pipe joint and replaced it in
its bed of foam packing. Susan resealed the box with
tape. The three of them worked feverishly after that,
Cantu opening boxes and extracting pipe joints, he
and Cruz stuffing them with currency, Susan taping
the boxes closed.

Involved in what they were doing, they neither
heard nor saw a figure slink into the storage area
from the dock area, and didn't suspect that a witness sat hunkered behind a row of boxes just yards
away from them.

They finished in just over an hour. "A job well
done," Cruz said as Susan soothed down the last
strip of tape. Again, the blatant suggestion in his eyes
made her feel dirty when he looked at her.

Refusing to give him the satisfaction of knowing
he was making her uncomfortable, she leveled a different sort of look at him. "I believe we have one bit
of business left, Señor Cruz."

He smiled enigmatically. "Such a lovely woman—
such a mercenary heart." He picked up the portfolio he'd carried in and opened it. "You like the sight
of money, no? One hundred and fifty thousand U.S.
dollars. Ten percent, as agreed. You may count it if
you like."

She couldn't have written a more incriminating script; his pompous pride was going to seal the case against him. "You appear to be a man of honor, Señor Cruz. I don't have to count it."

Lifting her hand to his lips, he kissed it gallantly. "With such a woman, a man must have honor."

Don't make me nauseous, Susan thought, beginning to feel the first hint of relief that everything had gone well and was almost over. To reinforce his perception of her, she retrieved her hand and ran it over the stacks of currency in the portfolio. "Not as warm as a man, but quite substantial."

Cruz laughed. "Logan is a lucky man to have such a clever woman. You are his mistress, no?"

"I am his mistress, yes."

"If this were not so, I would know you better."

"You flatter me." What the hell was going on— why didn't he just leave instead of playing all this verbal footsie? They were going to love this in the courtroom, and Peter was going to roll off his chair laughing when he saw the video.

Cruz lifted her hand again and kissed it one last time. "Goodbye, my new friend."

Susan waited until they were out of the door. Heaving a great sigh of relief, she closed the briefcase and carried it upstairs to Logan's office. Peter should arrive within minutes, and they would tag the case and the money as evidence and record the serial numbers of the bills.

Suddenly limp, she sank into the chair behind the desk, weak with relief. To think that Clark had almost . . .

"I'll take that bag, Steffie."

Logically Susan should have reacted with fear at the sight of the gun in Clark's hand. It was a big-barreled gun of gray metal. But Susan was too stunned for logic. In the face of Clark's betrayal, the gun seemed insignificant.

Chapter Ten

The betrayal ripped through her. His name tore from her throat, a miserable, discordant croak that elongated a single syllable into several.

"I tried to stop you," he said, "but you couldn't get past the cold, hard cash." He laughed, a bitter, ugly sound. "I was so wrong about you, Steffie. I thought I saw something in you besides Logan's mercenary mistress, willing to sell herself for a fancy car and an expense account. Tell me, is there a numbered bank account in Switzerland, too? Or are the Cayman Islands more your speed? The Caymans, I think. Hot tropics."

"Clark," she said again, like a parrot repeating the same word over and over. It was the only thing she could think to say, the only thing that reached through the shock and the shattering pain of a heart that was breaking.

"Aren't you going to deal, Steffie? We could get a long way from here on that much cash. Surely you'd be willing to sacrifice a little of yourself to keep it."

Unable to face him, she stared at the portfolio on the desk. "Please stop, Clark. If you want the money bad enough to...to kill me to get it, then take it. I don't give a damn about it."

Peter and his men weren't far away. They'd catch Clark easily enough. And, even if he should get away with the money, there was the incriminating video-tape to seal their case against the South American kingpin and his local operatives. The money couldn't be that important; nothing was important in the face of the fact that Clark had known about it, had been using her to get to it.

"I don't give a damn about the money either!" he said bitterly. He stared at the gun in his hand as though he'd forgotten he was holding it, almost as though it had sprouted there and he had only just noticed it. His shoulders sagged as he lowered his hand, and his arms hung loosely at his side. "God help me, Steffie, I don't care about the money."

The abrupt change in his demeanor was unnerving. Susan watched, mesmerized, as he sank into the chair opposite hers and said defeatedly, "There's no way around your being arrested, but—"

"Arrested?"

"This is your first offense, and there's a good chance you won't have to go to prison if you cooperate with us. If you'd help us hang the thugs who were just here—"

"Cruz and Cantu?" Susan's head was spinning. Too much was happening too quickly. She couldn't make sense of it, put everything into perspective.

"That's a girl, Steffie. Name names. We'll have them in custody soon, and your testimony..."

We'll have them in custody soon.... Susan's faculties returned to her in an avalanche of comprehension. He hadn't been *stealing* the money; he had been taking it into custody. And whatever agency he was working for was about to destroy the Task Force operation.

"Who are you working for?" she asked urgently.

"The good guys," he said glibly.

She got up, ran to him, heedless of the gun still clutched in his hand, and put her hands on his shoulders, willing him to look at her, heed her. "You can't arrest them. You mustn't. You have to stop—"

He shrugged her hands away. "Give it up, Steffie. You're caught, and they're as good as in prison. Play it smart and cooperate, and I'll do everything I can to help you."

"You don't understand!" she said. "I—"

"I think perhaps I could be of help."

Susan and Clark both turned toward the source of the voice. "He's got a gun, Peter," Susan warned.

"And I have a badge," Peter said coolly, holding it up as he walked toward them. "Agent Warshauer,

U.S. Drug Task Force." Then, as Clark seemed to shrink with the realization, he said, "Have a seat, Susan. Everything's under control."

"Susan?" Clark echoed incredulously.

"We've been in touch with your people at the D.A.'s office," Peter told Clark. "We had the phones hooked up for monitoring in case Cruz made any calls, and we were able to make the number you dialed."

"You're not Steffie Meeks?" Clark boomed, ignoring Peter. Susan stared back at him, an overwhelmed, confused, near-tears shine in her eyes. She understood his shock, the outrage. She understood it too well.

"We apprised them of the situation and canceled the bulletin on Cruz's car," Peter continued, unheard.

"Who *are* you?"

Unable to bear the confusion and anguish in his face, to face the accusation of betrayal in his eyes, Susan buried her face in her hands. How could she have thought he might just accept the fact that he'd been duped and forgive and forget? There was nothing real between them to salvage or build on; both of them had been illusory figures in fairy-tale daydreams.

"Mrs. Carlson is with Border Control," Peter said. "We recruited her because of her striking resemblance to Steffie Meeks."

Clark heard only the "Mrs." It landed like a billy club in his midsection, knocking the wind from him.

Peter, undaunted by the personal undercurrents churning in the room, chose to ignore them and get on with business. "Our audio was was perfect, Susan. If the video is half as good . . ."

He turned to Clark. "You gave us a few anxious moments when you showed up unexpectedly." Back to Susan, "We couldn't hear what was going on. We were damned glad when you came back into mike range and we could tell he was gone." His impatience to wrap up the job was obvious as he bobbed his head toward the door. "I want to get that videotape and take a look at what we've got."

Susan and Clark fell into step behind him, moving as stiffly as automatons, numbed by personal concerns. Still in shock over the shattering of the illusions Susan had created as Steffie, Clark watched without his characteristic curiosity as Peter opened the back of the camera crate and, after switching off the camera, ejected the cassette. He held it up in his hand as he might a hard-earned trophy and said to Susan, "A fine piece of work. Let's get over to the office and take a look at our handiwork."

He turned to Clark. "You need to contact your own people in the D.A.'s office, Haggerty, but before you leave, I have to stress the importance of discretion on this operation. The goal now is to keep this under wraps. Until we can grab our boy at the other end, everything has to go down exactly as it would have if none of us were involved. A rumor or tip-off could blow the entire setup."

Clark's eyes were on Susan as he answered Peter. There was a hardness in his voice so intense that it hurt Susan to hear it. "I think we've both proven that we can be discreet."

The dream ended just that quickly. No goodbyes, no farewell scenes. Clark simply turned and walked away while Susan and Peter went upstairs for her purse and the portfolio of money. His car was already out of the parking lot by the time she and Peter reached the Corvette.

"I'll drive," Peter said. "You look a little green around the gills."

Feeling more than just a little green around the gills, Susan nodded and handed him the keys. Once they were clear of the warehouse parking lot, he reached across the console to pat her hand paternally. "It's just the letdown after all the excitement. Perfectly normal after a job like this. It'll pass."

To her consternation, a tear fell on his hand, and he realized she was crying. It wasn't just the letdown from the job, she thought bitterly, remembering the shock registered on Clark's face when Peter had called her Susan. It was the end of a dream that wouldn't come true.

Minutes later, she said, "What do you know about him?"

"Haggerty?" Peter asked. "Not much. He had the experience profile to get the foreman job, so they let him go in to keep his eyes and ears open. They were just fishing. They weren't sure what they were looking for."

"Is he . . ." She couldn't finish the sentence.

"Married?" Peter guessed. He chanced a glance away from the traffic to look at her. "No. The only thing about his background he withheld at LIFT is that he's in his last semester of law school. He's applied for a full-time job with the D.A.'s office after graduation."

Law school, of course. The classes he took at night. The truth about him had been right before her eyes, and she hadn't seen it. She had been as gullible and ready to believe an illusion as he had.

"Look, Susan, I've been in this undercover business a long time," Peter said. "Things happen fast and they seem more intense when you're living in a specialized little world. But when you get back into the real world again, everything falls back into place and you regain your perspective. Maybe there's something between you and Haggerty. And then again, maybe there's not. Give yourself some time to get your perspective back before you do anything drastic."

Anything drastic? Susan thought. Like fling herself at his feet and beg him to forgive her for not being who and what he had believed her to be when all the time he hadn't been what he had appeared to be either? Fat chance! Strangely there should be a symmetry to the fact that they had been fooling each other, but the double treachery only compounded their separate deceptions.

* * *

The videotape was of excellent quality, and Peter praised Susan's work as exemplary. "If you should decide to do this work full-time, you'll get a glowing letter of recommendation from me."

"Nothing doing," Susan said. "I'm going home to hug my kids and check IDs at the bridge."

"I'll pick up the tab if you want to have your hair dyed back to its natural color," he offered.

"I don't think so," Susan said, as surprised by the impromptu decision as he. "I think I'll keep my apricot fizz as a souvenir, at least until the roots get so long that I have to do something about it."

"Are you sure you'd rather drive than fly? They have carriers for animals that go right on the airplane with you. We can make arrangements for the kitten."

"I really don't mind driving."

Before leaving, she walked through the condo one last time, pausing in the garden bathroom with its luxurious sunken tub. Sadness descended over her, and with it a bone weariness. The fantasy that had been so vivid evaporated now in the face of reality, banished to the same oblivion as the dream of confronting Clark with her true identity and having him accept Susan Carlson the way he'd accepted Steffie Meeks.

The long, tedious drive afforded her time and solitude for thinking. She thought of Clark, and of Peter's theory that everything was telescoped and warped out of perspective on an operation like the

one she'd been on. She remembered the sparkle i
Clark's eyes when he smiled his easy smile, the fee
of his arms around her. And then she recalled th
betrayal she'd felt when she'd thought he was steal
ing the money at gunpoint. The stunned look on hi
face when he'd learned she wasn't Steffie, the hurt i
his eyes, were etched permanently in her mind. Sh
could still hear the astonishment and disbelief in hi
voice as he'd asked plaintively, "Who are you?"

She wasn't sure what the answer to that questio
should be. She knew who she had been when she'
left home, and she understood the woman she ha
pretended to be, but she couldn't define who she wa
right now. She was Susan Carlson, yet she was a dif
ferent woman from the one Tyler Fannin had drive
to the airport just weeks earlier. The change might b
permanent, or it might be only a form of temporar
insanity—acute identity crisis brought on by immer
sion in an illusory world of light and shadow.

Seven hours of soul-searching in the rented ca
didn't net her any answers. If Clark should sud
denly appear before her and ask "Who *are* you?"
again, she still wouldn't have an answer for him.

The kids were playing outside when she pulled int
the driveway, and they eyed her speculatively unti
Kara recognized her and shouted, "It's Momma!"

In the midst of an orgy of hugging, they deluge
her with observations and questions. Did you hav
fun? Your hair looks funny. Did you miss us? Di
you bring us anything?

To this last, Susan responded with a smug smile and a drawn-out "Well-l-l."

"What is it?" Kara asked.

"I hope it's an Astros baseball hat," Greg Junior said.

She laughed and mussed his hair. "You've got plenty of baseball hats. I brought something really special."

The children loved the kitten instantly. "What's her name?" Kara asked, giggling as the kitten licked at her nose.

"Cuddles," Susan answered.

"I want to hold her," Greg Junior said. "Kara's already had a turn." It was enough to launch a full-scale argument, which Susan refereed.

The children's raised voices brought their grandmother to the door just as Susan was impressing them with the need for gentleness with the kitten, and Louise stepped outside to see who was talking to the children so familiarly.

Several seconds passed before she recognized Susan, and there was a beat of silence before she said, "Good grief, what have you done to your hair?"

"Moved into the eighties, Mother. Don't you like it? I've sorta gotten used to it."

Louise harrumphed skeptically. "Your daddy's going to bust a gusset."

"It won't be the first gusset he's busted, and it won't be the last. Busted gussets are rarely fatal."

"You're certainly a prickly cactus today. You haven't even said hello yet."

Susan threw her arms around her mother. "I'm sorry, Mom. I guess I'm just tired from the drive."

"Come on in and I'll get us some iced tea. I want to hear all about your trip."

They talked for some time. Louise heard about the color consultant who'd done Susan's hair, and about the garden bath in Steffie's condo and Steffie's pretty clothes. Susan told her about learning to handle the Corvette and about the tugboats that passed the windows at Shanghai Red's and about the musical at the Music Hall. She even told a carefully edited version of chasing Jezebel into the rafters and getting the kitten for the kids. What Susan studiously avoided was any specific mention of Clark Haggerty. She wasn't ready to talk about Clark to her mother. She wasn't sure she ever would be.

"You'd better call Tyler and let him know you're home," Louise said when the conversation had dwindled into silence. "He was planning on picking you up at the airport."

Reluctantly Susan nodded. "I suppose I should."

"You might as well ask him for dinner while you've got him on the phone. I've got a roast on, and your daddy was planning on eating over here anyway."

The last thing Susan needed tonight was an encounter with Tyler, but since she had to face him eventually, and she didn't feel like answering the inevitable questions her mother would ask if she balked at inviting him to dinner, she capitulated.

He arrived almost at the same time as her father.

Jake Owens remained steadfast in his absolute dislike of her new hairstyle, calling it unnatural and "all fussied up," but Tyler, with ulterior motives for not wanting to raise Susan's ire, was more diplomatic and said, "It'll take some getting use to," even though the tone of his voice was less than convincing when he said it.

Dreading having to deal with Tyler after her parents left, Susan had little appetite for the meat-and-potatoes meal her mother had prepared. The children, bless them, chattered so animatedly about their new pet that no one seemed to notice her distractedness.

At bedtime there was a heated argument over which child the kitten would sleep with, which Susan settled by announcing that Cuddles would sleep in a box in the kitchen. Then, after collecting an extra hug from each child to make up for all those she'd missed while she was away, she was able to get them tucked in for the night.

"Are they asleep?" Tyler asked when she returned to the living room. He'd settled in the reclining chair that had been Greg's favorite and was reading the newspaper. It grated on Susan's nerves that he appeared so comfortable there, almost as though he were invading her privacy and Greg's memory by making himself so at home.

"They're on their way," she said, sitting down on the sofa that sagged where she'd sat repeatedly over the years.

"They missed you."

"I missed them."

"I missed you."

"I missed you, too, Tyler."

The ensuing silence grew long and, determined to end it, they each said the other's name at precisely the same moment, then laughed self-consciously. "Ladies first," Tyler said, and she thought what a Tylerian gesture that was, so studiously, predictably gallant.

"I've been doing a lot of thinking about us, Tyler," she said bluntly. "It's not going to work."

He came to attention, springing the recliner into its upright position. "But we've got so much in common."

"Maybe that's the problem. Maybe we're too much alike."

"People should have things in common. It's the ideal basis for a marriage."

"We don't just have things in common, Tyler, we have *everything* in common. There's no room for either of us to be an individual. We'd just meld into one lump of a personality."

"Marriage is supposed to be a union, to make two people one."

"Physically, yes. That's the Biblical term, isn't it, to become 'as one'? But intellectually people should complement each other, not overlap. We'd stop growing and end up just boring each other into old age."

"I could never be bored with you."

She shrugged. "Not bored, maybe, but complacent. We're already complacent with each other.
That's why we've been seeing each other as long as
we have. It's been convenient for both of us. I've had
pleasant company and an escort without having to
face the risks of dating, and you haven't had to deal
with the possibility of getting hurt again." Tyler had
been engaged once, genuinely in love, and his fian-
cée had broken off the engagement just weeks before the wedding.

He looked at her as though she'd turned into a
stranger. As, perhaps, she had. "I've never known
you to be cynical before."

"Oh, Tyler, can't you see that we've been using
each other? Which is okay. Friends are allowed to use
each other occasionally when they need a boost. But
only temporarily. It's time for us to move in separate directions. Greg's been dead for two years, and
it's time for me to take a few gambles in the romance department. As for you, Tyler," she said,
glowering at him authoritatively, "you've got to quit
running from that passel of women who hang
around hoping you'll notice them. You've got to find
someone to settle down with."

"What's gotten into you, Susan? First your hair,
and now this burr under your saddle...."

"Nothing's gotten into me, Tyler. I just... when
I was away, I was able to see things from a different
perspective."

"I'll be damned!" he said. "You met a man."

Susan had had her fill of subterfuge and decep
tion and didn't even try to deny the allegation. He
silence confirmed the truth of it as surely as a verba
admission.

"I'll be damned!" he said again.

Indignantly Susan said, "You don't have to act a
though it were the last thing in the world you coul
expect to happen. If *you* find me...whatever it is yo
find me...why is it so hard to believe some other ma
might be attracted to me?"

He moved to the sofa and took her hand. "It's no
hard to imagine men attracted to you, Susan. Me
notice you all the time. I see them watching you whe
I'm with you." He smiled sweetly. "It always make
me feel proud. Important. I'm just surprised yo
noticed a man."

"You mean it's surprising that Susie Cuke migh
have warm blood flowing in her veins."

"What on earth are you talking about?"

"They call me that on the bridge," she said. "Su
sie Cuke, short for cucumber. It's their way of spec
ulating on the limitations of my libido."

"Oh, for crying out loud, Susan! It's just a stupi
nickname. You shouldn't pay any attention to thing
like that."

Susan wanted to cry out loud. She needed to cry
and cry she did, on the reliable pillow of Tyler'
shoulder, while Tyler patted her back and whispered
assurances in her ear.

"I'm sorry," she sniffed when she had regained her composure. "I've been a bundle of nerves since I got back. I think it's like jet lag, only I didn't fly."

"Why don't you tell me about him."

Wiping her cheek with her fingers, she looked at Tyler with red-rimmed eyes.

"If I have to lose you to some city slicker, the least you can do is tell me all about him," he prompted.

"Oh, Tyler," she said, succumbing to a fresh wave of tears, "there's nothing to tell. That's the worse part. There's nothing to tell."

He wrapped his arms around her as he would a child. "Poor Susan. He's broken your heart." Then he added gravely, "And now you're going to break mine."

She sat up, pulling herself out of his arms. "I don't like hurting you, Tyler, but you've got to see that we've been leaning on each other to keep from getting hurt, and now we've got to let go before we make a terrible mistake."

"I've got to let go before *you* make a terrible mistake. I would like to marry you, Susan, and you know how I feel about your children. But if it wouldn't make you happy, then it would be wrong."

She smiled sadly. "You know how much I value your friendship. I wouldn't want to lose it."

He threw his arm across her shoulders and gave her a bear hug. "Your kids have an uncle for life. But you have to realize that you might lose your mother over this."

She laughed, and the tension between them dissolved. Why hadn't she realized that Tyler was nothing if not a good sport? "She's stuck with me no matter how irrational she thinks I am," she said. "I'm her only child."

Brownsville never changed, Susan reflected as she traveled the familiar route from the house to the border station. It was the same sleepy little town it always had been, dear to her because it was home, comforting because of its constancy. Home had embraced her upon her return, welcoming her back to familiar sights and established routines, yet she wasn't content. She found herself vaguely dissatisfied, gripped by an air of expectancy, as though she were waiting for something remarkable to happen.

Peter called to let her know the kingpin was in custody and, several days later, called again to tell her Cruz and Cantu had been indicted by the grand jury on the basis of the physical evidence against them. Her job had been done thoroughly and well.

But there'd been no showdown, no resolution with Clark Haggerty. Where he was concerned, she was nagged by a feeling of having left something unfinished. She hadn't gone to find him in search of a showdown, though she should have, and he hadn't come to her that last day at the condo, though he could have.

The dream of an honest relationship with him hadn't faded with gradual wakefulness; it had dissolved in a single *poof!* as though she'd been jarred

awake abruptly. Susan was beginning to believe it
would have been better if the two of them had gone
after each other in a frank confrontation, growling
and snarling like pit bulls, rather than leaving everything unsettled between them. Losing Clark was
tragic enough, but the pain of leaving him without
ever having had an honest exchange with him was
particularly painful.

The process of relegating Clark Haggerty to the
status of a sweet memory turned out to be a perversely slow one. Vivid images of him invaded her
mind with dogged perseverance: the sparkle in his
eyes as he smiled, the small scar on his cheek, the
large, strong hands that were quick enough to catch
a wild cat and gentle enough to play with a kitten.
Hands that had touched her lovingly, reminding her
of her womanhood and arousing womanly needs in
her.

Remembering him, she longed for him, and telling herself she had to forget him only made her long
for him more. In a thousand daydreams she went to
him or he came to her and they forgave and forgot
deceptions; they recalled the magic of the evening
they'd spent on Steffie's small balcony watching the
stars; recalled the sweetness of their good-night kiss
that night, the poignant pain of their parting when
they'd wanted so desperately to stay together.

Recognizing the daydreams for what they were,
Susan lost hold of the hope that they might come
true. Still, she wondered if Clark daydreamed about
her, and if he recognized, after the fact, that her re-

fusal to go to bed with him had been a form of honesty, an avoidance of an ultimate, unforgivable deception. *Did he know—would he allow himself to believe—that she had fallen in love with him?*

Did he care?

Deep down inside her, some optimistic, romantic part of her refused to believe that he wouldn't care. There had been an undeniable truth in his kisses, honesty in his touch, genuine anguish in his eyes when he'd learned she wasn't the person he'd believed her to be.

She took refuge in routine. For a day, a week, several weeks she awoke to the grating squeal of the alarm clock and did what had to be done: caring for the kids, her job at the bridge, the laundry, the dishes. Routine became a Band-Aid that hid the ache of missing Clark while she waited for her wounded spirit to heal.

While soaking in a bathtub that was small and produced no bubbles, she decided that Clark Haggerty was an affliction she must let pass through her system, one from which she might never fully recover but whose effects she might overcome, as she might learn to maneuver a damaged knee after an injury.

Until then she would just continue cloaking herself in routine and avoiding her mother and the inevitable questions about her breakup with Tyler.

Chapter Eleven

Greg Junior had math homework every Tuesday night. He had his binder and book spread out on one side of the breakfast nook table while Kara played with modeling clay on the other.

"Kara's wobbling the table," he said.

"I am not!"

Susan looked up from the sink where she was washing the dishes that didn't fit in the dishwasher. "Try to be a little gentler when you pat the clay, Kara."

"I wasn't wobbling the table!"

"You were, too."

"I'm sure you weren't jiggling the table on purpose," Susan told her daughter, "but you were patting the clay pretty hard. Just be careful."

The cease-fire, tenuous at best, lasted less than a minute before Greg complained, "She's doing it again."

"I am not! Momma, he's lying."

Susan looked at them and sighed in exasperation. Nothing was ever simple with children! "Move your clay over here to the counter."

"But—"

"Now. Or go take your bath and get ready for bed."

"It's not fair!" Kara said, collecting her cans of clay.

The doorbell rang. "I'll get it!" the children cried in unison, leaping up.

"Let Kara get it," Susan told Greg. "You need to finish your homework." He shot her a disgruntled scowl and settled back into his chair.

Kara sashayed to the front door and returned almost immediately. "It's a man, Mommy. He wants to talk to you."

Susan turned to see who it was just as Clark, following Kara, rounded the corner to the breakfast nook. She stood stock-still for several seconds, and he grinned self-consciously. "Hello, Susan."

"Clark," she said, and added lamely, "Hello."

"I hope I didn't come at a bad time."

"Not at all. We just finished dinner."

Over the heads of the children they conversed without words, posing questions with their eyes: What are you doing here? Was it all right for me to come?

"I haven't met your children," he said.

"Greg, Kara," Susan said, "This is Mr. Haggerty."

The children's reserved hellos were accompanied by evaluative, curious perusals. Clark extended his hand to Greg as he would to an adult.

Unsure how Greg would react, Susan watched as a blush spread over his face. But he took Clark's hand and shook it, and Susan could tell he was pleased to be treated in a grown-up fashion. "What are you working on?" Clark asked, nodding toward Greg's binder and textbook.

"Math," Greg said, screwing up his face. "Fractions."

"I remember fractions," Clark answered. "They're pretty tricky."

Kara, feeling left out of the camaraderie, stepped as close to Clark as she dared and said, "I made a turtle. And a mushroom and an alligator."

"Let me see," Clark said, chancing a look at Susan over Kara's head as he walked to the counter. She was leaning against the counter with her arms akimbo, dish towel still in her hand, watching Clark with the children as she would a movie. The expression on her face was so full of perplexity that he wished he dared to hug her.

"See," Kara said, tugging at his hand, drawing his attention to her clay sculptures.

"Very nice," he said. "Do they have names?"

"His name is Pokey," she said, obviously ad-libbing as she pointed at the turtle. "And this is Alley, short for alligator."

"I should have known. Pokey and Alley. Are you going to be an artist when you grow up, Kara?"

The child glowed in the light of his flattery. Male flattery, which she hadn't gotten much of since Tyler had quit dropping in every other day. "No. I'm going to be a movie star."

"I see," Clark said, grinning at her precocity. "Well, you're certainly pretty enough—you look a lot like your mommy."

"Except I still have blond hair," Kara said, "and my hair's curly."

"Did you mom's hair used to be blond?"

Kara looked at him as though she though him very stupid. "Until she went away to Houston and got it dyed."

Thanks loads, Susan thought. "It's time to put away the clay and get your bath," she said.

"Oh, Mom," Kara said. "Can't I make one more animal?"

"Just one?" Clark interjected, adopting the child's pleading tone.

Susan would have liked to scrub the grin from his face with her dish towel. "Ten minutes," she said.

"What'll we make?" Clark asked Kara, and they were soon absorbed in the creation of a grizzly bear.

"I don't understand this," Greg said. "Mom."

Susan sat down next to him, read the problem he was working on and picked up his textbook. "Let's

see, first you have to find the common denomina-
tor. With three and five, that would be fifteen. How
many fifteenths would four-fifths be?''

A few grueling problems later, she looked up while
Greg was wrestling with converting a whole number
into thirty-seconds. "How's that bear coming
along?''

"Just putting on the finishing touches," Clark
answered.

"It's real scary," Kara added.

"It sure is," Susan agreed. "Are you going to let
it harden so you can keep it?''

"Yeah!''

"Then leave it on the counter, but put the rest of
the clay away.''

Kara did as she was told. Then she walked over to
Susan and put a small hand on her mother's shoulder. "Will you start my bathwater?''

"Sure, babe, if Mr. Haggerty will excuse us.''

"Of course," Clark said.

"What do you say to Mr. Haggerty for helping
you make the bear?" Susan prompted.

"Thank you," Kara said. Later, in the bathroom,
she opined, "Mr. Haggerty's nice.''

"Yes," Susan agreed. "Very nice.''

"He thinks you're pretty.''

Susan smiled. "He said that, didn't he?" She was
still reeling with the knowledge that Clark was here,
in Brownsville, in her home.

"He thinks I'm pretty, too.''

"Yes, he does. Pretty enough to be a movie star.''

The taps were adjusted to the right temperature, and the tub was filling. Susan helped Kara get the snug neck of her T-shirt over her head. "Is he your boyfriend? The way Tyler was?"

Susan hesitated, not sure how to answer the direct question. Inside she was tingling with a resurgence of hope. He had come all the way to Brownsville to see her. "He's a special friend, Kara. We worked together when I was in Houston."

"Is that why he didn't know your hair was blond?"

"Uh-huh," Susan said, feigning nonchalance so Kara would drop the subject. "I'll get your nightshirt. Don't forget to scrub your knees."

Returning to the breakfast nook, she found Clark and Greg head-to-head over Greg's homework. "How's the math coming?" she asked.

"I'm on the last problem," Greg said. "Mr. Haggerty's been helping me."

"Mr. Haggerty seems to be a handy man to have around," she said, her eyes fixing on Clark's.

By the time Greg had packed his binder and books into his backpack for school, Kara was out of the tub, her face flushed from her bath, hair damp around the edges, angelic in her pink knit sleep shirt. Susan scooted Greg off to take his bath and escorted Kara to bed, then, with Kara tucked in, hurried Greg out of the bath and into his bed.

Before returning to the living room, where she had instructed Clark to make himself at home, she took a deep breath for courage, unsure whether she was more afraid of what Clark would say or what he wouldn't.

He was sitting on the sofa when she returned, scanning the room interestedly, and she wondered if he was comparing it to Steffie's condo and finding it lacking. He stood up when he heard her approaching.

He sensed her defensiveness and wished he knew how to put her at ease. "This is a pleasant room," he said, meaning it. "Comfortable."

Susan laughed nervously. "Lived in, you mean. It's not like the condo, all shiny and new."

"It's more comfortable than the condo—cozier."

She had stopped several feet from him. "What are you doing in Brownsville?"

He could hear the insecurity, the anxiety in her voice. Giving rein to his instincts, he got up and walked over to her and put his hands on the tops of her shoulders. Slowly she tilted her head up to look at him, almost as though she were afraid to face what she would find in his eyes.

He marveled at how she could break his heart open with just a look, open it and find the tenderness hidden there. "I was confused," he said. "I needed to see you. By the time I was over the shock of your being an agent, you were gone. Why did you leave, Susan?"

"Everything was so convoluted. Do you realize you spent most of the time we were together trying to talk me out of my life of sin?"

He slid his arms around her. "Because I wanted you, and Logan didn't deserve you."

Susan wanted to relax into the strength of his solid body, to lose herself in the oblivion of the warm, wonderful sensations he evoked in her, but she didn't dare. Not yet.

"You must know I'm in love with you," he said.

She wanted to believe him, but she couldn't until she was sure he knew which woman he was talking to. "You fell in love with an illusion. The glamorous Steffie Meeks. Logan's mistress. Look at me, Clark. Blue jeans, a small house with worn furniture, kids. I just was a surface imitation of Steffie Meeks."

"No, Susan. You're wrong. It was you."

"How can you be sure?"

"I met Steffie Meeks. She was a poor imitation of you."

Susan's head jerked back so she could see his face. "You met her?"

He tightened his arms around her, pulling her closer. "There was a physical resemblance, but it ended there. It was like looking at a life-size poster of you—I could admire her beauty, but I wasn't stimulated by it."

He stroked her cheek with the backs of his fingers, enjoying the softness of her skin, while his eyes caressed her face. "Your eyes are blue."

"Very little about me is the same as Steffie."

He hugged her again, urgently. "Don't you know that Steffie doesn't matter? It was Susan Carlson I fell in love with. Names and cars and condos—even your eye color—are all irrelevant. What matters is what I see inside you when I look into your eyes.''

Susan was letting go of her reservations, beginning to trust, letting herself believe that lost dreams could be reclaimed. Her lips were slightly parted, voluptuous, waiting for his kiss, and with utmost gentleness he lowered his own lips to them, not wanting to rush, wanting instead to savor the remembered sweetness of her.

He found that sweetness in her surrender, in the way she slid her arms around his waist, snuggled her body against his as his kiss grew more demanding, and then nestled her cheek against his chest and sighed when his lips left hers. There was something basic and innocent in the utter femininity of her response to him that made him feel like a man—strong, powerful, almost invincible—and that stirred some basic instinct in him to hug her close against him and shield her from harm.

He stroked her hair, silky against his palm, as he breathed in the scent of it, not exotic like the perfume she had used as Steffie, but light and fresh-smelling, conveying the same unaffected innocence as her smile. ''I want to know you, Susan. Everything about you.''

Still afraid to believe in the dream, she pulled away from him. ''How much did Peter tell you?''

''You know federal agents. The sketchiest details. The first thing I asked about was your marital status.''

"He told you I'm a widow."

"Yes. And for a while it was like being released from prison, like leaving a dark cell to dance in the sunlight. And then I felt guilty, as though I were celebrating your husband's death, dancing on his grave." He desperately needed to touch her, for courage, to reestablish the contact they'd lost when she'd stepped out of his arms. He reached up, combed his fingers through her hair. She closed her eyes, inhaling sharply as his hand cupped her scalp, and a subtle nudge brought her back to him, into his arms where she belonged. Where he wanted and needed her.

He kissed her again urgently, because for a moment he'd lost her and it had frightened him. Afterward, he hugged her. "I was confused, even driving down here. It was so much to deal with. But the moment I saw you again, standing at the sink, with your kids sprawled all over the room with their toys and schoolbooks, all the confusion evaporated."

He was rocking her in his arms, cradling her head against his chest. "Tell me that names don't matter to you, either, that you felt what was happening between us, too."

"I felt it. It was real."

Something tinged the blunt sincerity of her words, something ominous and threatening, fingers of an unknown enemy closing around Clark's chest, taking his breath away. "You hesitated," he said.

Again she stepped back, away from him, as though she were afraid to let herself touch him too long. "What about my children, Clark?"

"That's one reason it took me so long to get up my courage to come. Quite frankly I had to do a lot of thinking about it. Loving you was one thing, but children..."

"You came anyway," she said, with a note of wonder in her voice.

"It wasn't an easy decision. Not one I took lightly."

"What exactly did you decide?"

"That the way I feel about you is so special that nothing else matters. I had to see if you felt the same way, if you wanted to try to make it work."

His eyes searched hers, looking for an answer. "You have such beautiful eyes," he said. "I always felt I could look inside you through your eyes. Tell me now that what I'm seeing is love, that I'm not imagining it there because I want so desperately to see it."

"I do love you," she said. "I'm just... it's hard for me to believe you're here, saying what I've dreamed so often of hearing you say."

"It's a little hard for me to believe, too. To be honest with you, I'm scared to death."

A smile as bright as sunshine spread over her entire face and twinkled in her eyes. "I think I love you more at this moment than ever before." She touched his cheek with her fingertips, tracing the small scar under his eye. Then, standing on tiptoe, she kissed it.

"Any man who could fall off a roof playing cowboys and Indians when he's ten years old doesn't have to be afraid of children. You'll get along with them just fine."

"I wasn't worried about getting along with them, Susan." He captured her hand in his and pressed it to his lips. "I knew if they were your children they would have to be nice people. And I'm not exactly an ogre. In fact, I have seven nieces and nephews who happen to think their uncle Clark is something of a hero."

"Then it's the commitment you're afraid of."

He slipped his arm around her waist and hugged her. "No. Not exactly. Oh, Susan, I wish I could explain it to you, the reason I wasn't here weeks ago."

"Why don't we sit down. You can try."

"Sit next to me." She did, resting her head in the crook of his shoulder while he gathered the courage to bare his soul to her. It took him several moments to decide how to begin. Susan didn't prod or coax, just waited patiently, giving him her support through the silent communication of touch.

"Have you ever seen something that you didn't know you needed and suddenly knew you needed it?" he asked abruptly.

"I'm not sure I know what you mean."

"Suppose you had a wall, and it was a nice wall, painted a pretty color, and for years you were perfectly happy with that wall just plain. And then one day you're out shopping and you see a picture, and you know that picture is exactly right for that wall.

Suddenly you know that if you don't have that picture, the wall just won't be right anymore. But until you saw the picture, you never knew the wall needed anything.''

"I felt that way about a necklace once," she said. "It was a tiny heart with a diamond on it. When I saw it, I knew I couldn't go to the prom without it. And I hadn't even picked out my dress yet."

"That's the way I feel about you, Susan, like there'll be a great big hole in my life if you're not sharing it with me. I don't have anything to offer you except that. Up to now I've been drifting through life, and I haven't stopped to build anything. I quit college halfway through and joined the army, and since then I've been wandering from job to job while I finished school. And now I'm about to launch a new career. I'm a beginner at thirty-four. I don't have any business asking a woman to trust my stability, much less to entrust her children to me."

"It's enough," Susan said.

"I don't even have a job yet. I applied at the district attorney's office in Houston, but I didn't think you'd want to upset the kids by moving, so I applied at the district attorney's office here today, and I have an interview tomorrow, but . . ."

"Clark."

". . . there's no guarantee I'll be hired there, and I might have to go into private practice, and it could take years to get really established . . ."

"Clark."

"...but I know I can succeed, Susan. The only reason I haven't yet is that I haven't applied myself because I didn't have any incentive, but now—"

She sat up straight. "Clark!"

He was stunned into silence at the sharpness of her voice. "It's enough," she said. "Your love is enough for me. Everything else is like the car and the condo and the green contact lenses—it's all irrelevant. If you love me and like my kids, then the rest will fall into place."

"It's just... I don't have anything to offer—"

"You're forgetting that I worked with you. I know what a good man you are, even if you don't."

"But—"

"Are you trying to talk me out of marrying you?"

"Of course not. I just—"

"Then shut up and kiss me."

"Susan—"

"Talk's cheap, Haggerty. It's time for action. And if you don't kiss me right this very minute, I'm going to go stark raving mad."

His arms slid around her and gathered her to him. "They'd have to bring two straitjackets," he said.

It was the last thing he said for a very long time.

Thank you for shopping at the Book Rack. Please come again.

COMING NEXT MONTH

TAKES A THIEF—Rita Rainville

hen Dani Clayton broke into the wrong office at the wrong casino,
e was caught—by devastating Rafe Sutherland. Dani was
termined to get to the right place; Rafe was determined to keep her
t. Two such strong-willed people just *had* to fall in love.

PEARL BEYOND PRICE—Lucy Gordon

ot even the barriers from their pasts could prevent the sparks that
ew between Renato and Lynette. Renato was a hard man—would he
er understand the pricelessness of Lynette's love?

HOT PURSUIT—Pepper Adams

cret Service Agent J. P. Tucker had been trailing Maggie Ryan for
eks. But it wasn't until after he'd rescued her from kidnappers and
unterfeiters, and was chased all over the state, that he realized there
s more to shy Maggie than met the eye!

GH RIDER—Olivia Ferrell

deo clown Rama Daniels wanted a stable home life, and she was
re she couldn't have one with Barc Lawson. Barc was a rodeo rider,
nomad. Though he professed he was ready to settle down, Rama
ew rodeo was in his blood. Could he ever convince her otherwise?

EARTS ON FIRE—Brenda Trent

enna Johnson had always wanted to be a firefighter, and now she
d her chance. She knew she could put out the fires, but could she
ndle the burning glances of station captain Reid Shelden?

IE LEOPARD TREE—Valerie Parv

er first UFO! Tanith had always wanted to see one, and now she
d. But was the mysterious, compelling stranger who arrived with it
en or human? Evidence said alien, but her heart said he was very
ich a man.

AILABLE THIS MONTH:

ATTRACTIVE, SPACE SAVIN
BOOK RACK

Display your most prized novels on this handsome an
sturdy book rack. The hand-rubbed walnut finish wi
blend into your library decor with quiet elegance, pro
viding a practical organizer for your favorite hard-or sof
covered books.

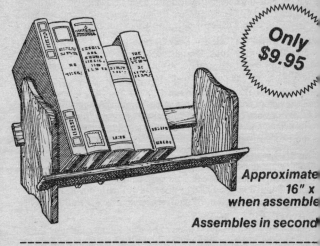

*Only
$9.95*

*Approximate
16" x
when assemble*

Assembles in second

To order, rush your name, address and zip code, alor
with a check or money order for $10.70* ($9.95 plus 75
postage and handling) payable to *Silhouette Books.*

Silhouette Books
Book Rack Offer
901 Fuhrmann Blvd.
P.O. Box 1325
Buffalo, NY 14269-1325

Offer not available in Canada.

*New York residents add appropriate sales tax.

Take 4 Silhouette Special Edition novels
FREE

and preview future books in your home for 15 days!

When you take advantage of this offer, you get 4 Silhouette Special Edition® novels FREE and without obligation. Then you'll also have the opportunity to preview 6 brand-new books —delivered right to your door for a FREE 15-day examination period—as soon as they are published.

When you decide to keep them, you pay just $1.95 each ($2.50 each in Canada) *with no shipping, handling, or other charges of any kind!*

Romance *is* alive, well and flourishing in the moving love stories of Silhouette Special Edition novels. They'll awaken your desires, enliven your senses, and leave you tingling all over with excitement... and the first 4 novels are yours to keep. You can cancel at any time.

As an added bonus, you'll also receive a FREE subscription to the Silhouette Books Newsletter as long as you remain a member. Each issue is filled with news on upcoming books, interviews with your favorite authors, even their favorite recipes.

To get your 4 FREE books, fill out and mail the coupon today!

Silhouette Special Edition®

Silhouette Books, 120 Brighton Rd., P.O. Box 5084, Clifton, NJ 07015-5084

**Clip and mail to: Silhouette Books,
120 Brighton Road, P.O. Box 5084, Clifton, NJ 07015-5084 •**

YES. Please send me 4 FREE Silhouette Special Edition novels. Unless you hear from me after I receive them, send me 6 new Silhouette Special Edition novels to preview each month. I understand you will bill me just $1.95 each, a total of $11.70 (in Canada, $2.50 each, a total of $15.00), with no shipping, handling, or other charges of any kind. There is no minimum number of books that I must buy, and I can cancel at any time. The first 4 books are mine to keep.

B1SS87

Name _____ (please print)

Address _____ Apt. #

City _____ State/Prov. _____ Zip/Postal Code

* In Canada, mail to: Silhouette Canadian Book Club, 320 Steelcase Rd., E., Markham, Ontario, L3R 2M1, Canada
Terms and prices subject to change.   SE-SUB-1A
SILHOUETTE SPECIAL EDITION is a service mark and registered trademark.

ELIZABETH QUINN

ALLIANCES

**They were allies, heart and soul.
Some would survive, some would die—
all would change.**

A young American war correspondent is able to face the
harsh realities of WWII and the emptiness of her own life
with the help of friends and lovers—alliances of the heart

Available in MARCH, or reserve your copy for February shipping by sending
your name, address, zip or postal code along with a check or money order for
$4.70 (includes 75¢ for postage and handling) payable to Worldwide Library
to:

In the U.S.A.	In Canada
Worldwide Library	Worldwide Library
901 Fuhrmann Blvd.	P.O. Box 609
Box 1325	Fort Erie, Ontario
Buffalo, NY 14269-1325	L2A 9Z9

Please specify book title with your order.

 **WORLDWIDE LIBRARY**   AL-